THE SONG OF THE SLEEPERS
A NOVELLA

THE CELESTIAL TEARS OF DYING LIGHT

JOSHUA WALKER

and Burrowers that warms your heart, even when a few pages later, Walker might devastate you with unexpected heartbreak.

Dave Lawson, Author of *The Envoys of War*

A captivating story of courage and resilience, set in a beautiful world that is brilliantly realised ... Walker has given us an appetiser that leaves you begging for dinner.

Scott Palmer, Author of *A Memory of Song*

Josh Walker weaves poetic prose into a beautifully immersive world that will instantly pull you in.

Isaac Hill, Author of *The Dragon Legion*

Both timelines weave together seamlessly, as one posits questions the other answer ... to demonstrate that Q'ara is large, living world full of magic and mystery.

Livia J Elliot, Author of *The Genesis of Change*

An enchanting Coming of Age tale about found family and the challenges of loss, sacrifice, and duty. Walker has once again crafted a dazzling masterpiece.

Kristen Shafer, SFF Insiders

The ability to craft a tone for not only the settings but the characters throughout, is masterful. The prose is rich, tactile, and effortless to read.

Vivian, Goodreads Reviewer

Blending the past and present in a seamless narrative, this story keeps you on the edge of your seat, offering thrilling twists and captivating moments at every turn.

Carina, Goodreads Reviewer

BY JOSHUA WALKER

The Song of the Sleepers

0.5) The Rest to the Gods

1) An Exile of Water & Gold

1.5) The Child of the Greenwood

2) An Empire of Dirt & Lies *(Forthcoming)*

2.5) The Celestial Tears of Dying Light

3) A Chorus of Light & Death *(Forthcoming)*

Tales from Q'ara (Standalone Novels)

The Tea-Gardens of Tel-Kathan *(Forthcoming)*

Loaves & Larceny *(Forthcoming)*

Edited by Sarah Chorn, https://sarahchornedits.com.

Proofread by Isabelle Wagner, https://theshaggyshepherd.wordpress.com.

Cover art and design by Stefanie Saw, https://www.seventhstarart.com.

Map design by Joshua Hoskins, Noctua Cartography (@Noctua_Maps).

Chapter Headings by Joshua Walker.

ISBN 978-1-7638435-1-6 (ebook)

ISBN 978-1-7638435-2-3 (paperback)

ISBN 978-1-7638435-3-0 (hardback)

To those who ask, 'What if?',
Hindsight's 20/20. It can be merciless, but it also be your silver lining.
The only way is up.

Contents

STOP!

Dear reader,

You thought I was going to put a heavy foot down about my absolutely unquestionable British English grammar, didn't you? Well, it's your lucky day, because this time, I have a different message for you.

Before we begin, I must warn you that *The Celestial Tears of Dying Light* contains many strong spoilers for *The Song of the Sleepers,* and the Luminous Earth it is set on as a whole.

If you have not read *The Rest to the Gods, The Child of the Greenwood,* or *An Exile of Water & Gold,* I strongly recommend you do so before embarking on your journey with Prisma and Nalor on the pages that follow.

If you have read any of those, buckle yourself in: you're in for a wild ride.

Josh

Sethi Ranges
Lake Sethiliquin
Ghabbat
The Rocklands
Piat
Ther
The Hidden Forest
Providence
Aobia
The Heart
The Viaduct

Port Town
To Ha'ar
The Heartstring
Adira River
The Outfields
Adira
Relond
The Continent of Q'ara

"Every trail has its end, and every calamity brings its lesson!"

\- James Fenimore Cooper, *The Last of the Mohicans*

★

"There is a layer of space between this world and another. Not the next, not the afterlife … but a vast infinitude of stars that have reclaimed the souls of our people. The ones who burned out live on, and they dwell above us all. Tala, with your daughters and sons, bless us."

—*The Book of Songs*, Aobian recorded histories.

PRISMA

Early Autumn, 2055 AS

PRISMA HUNCHED OVER THE desk built into the branchrendered wall of her apartment in the Mind of the Great Tree. On the desktop lay *The Book of Songs,* an Aobian recorded history she had found and asked permission to borrow from the Archives. Once an institution of Aobian history, *The Book of Songs* was now no more than a handful of catalogued copies that were considered propaganda. She had clearance to take out a copy in accordance with her position as a Sleeper, but was expected to return it once she had made it back home. From the day she'd arrived back in her country to the day she was to leave again, she would pore over every word with blood, sweat, and tears and record notes from the book in her personal journal, a loosely bound notebook of parchment. The worst part about leaving was not being there for the ones she loved, those she had sworn to protect. *My sister, my child, my beloved.* She shook the thought away.

The assignment she had been given was no small task; in fact, it scared her perhaps more than death itself. She was to willingly be cut off from the Tree, to venture as far north as any Aobian had ever gone … or so they thought. Staril's interest had been obvious when Prisma had been called to meet with the Twelve. "We believe there is evidence of another living Great Tree, north of Ghabbat," the prime minister had said, "and given the way the war ended, we are confident Therador will be hunting the same lead."

Prisma relived the conversation whenever she glanced down at *The Book of Songs.* It was said to hold the answer to many of Q'ara's secrets, and thus, the Magisterium had removed it from circulation after the collapse of the monarchy. Therador's hunt for the grindels—Luminous objects—scattered throughout Q'ara was aggressive and unstoppable. The Twelve had made it clear that the last, and most notable, grindel, while shrouded in mythology, was Veil-Piercer, a kind of *cism* said to hold vast amounts of power. The Twelve believed it could be real and perhaps give them answers about the potential Tree in the north: why nobody from there had ever corresponded with people south of Ghabbat, and why Therador was constantly in pursuit of these objects. But the information they truly wanted was to do with Veil-Piercer itself. It was said to contain Luminosity so great that it existed in some sort of in-between state.

"You will need to do this alone, Prisma," Koln, one of the Twelve, had said. "Nischia is not to know about this mission. The containment of whatever you find out there is to be of the utmost priority. Anything you discover about the lingering nature of supernova events must be treated as confidential, even upon your return."

"Why me?" Prisma gulped. It felt like a prison sentence. "I've only just returned from the battle, and now you ask me to leave my home, possibly forever. What offence have I made against the Magisterium?"

"None, child," Loche had replied. Her superior. The one who had eased her into this life, who had taught her what it meant to be a leader and a Sleeper for Aobia. Even he was condemning her. "But I believe you are the only one called on this journey. Perhaps, if you accept this request, you will discover why."

That had been that. When she had been away, fighting at the Mountain Pass with Nischia and the Hidden Ones, she had hungered to return home; the Tree seemed to have a tether to her heart. She felt older, somehow, and ached with a deep melancholy, like she was a pet cast aside by her master. *It's like we are puppets and our strings have snapped,* Prisma thought. It was no matter, though. She had accepted the assignment to go to Ghabbat and would be gone by the end of the week. She sighed and stared down at the pages before her, hoping something written on them would distract her from her woes.

Tala believed we came from all corners of the continent, though the people she had led to the Tree never acknowledged this. Not until the day that two foreign visitors arrived via a raft that had made its way downstream on the River Tomei. For weeks, the female and her son could not communicate with Tala or her advisors. But slowly, Tala learned many of the foreigners' words. In her wisdom, she concluded that one word specifically was translated to mean 'escape'. Frustrated that she could not find a way to ask them from where they had fled, she laid out a pressed-parchment map of Aobia and the Janub desert. The visitor and her son looked confused. The mother shook her head and said something unfamiliar. Tala tapped the paper again, urging them to look. Then, the mother drew her finger from the River Tomei beside the Great Tree and moved it up, off the page. From somewhere in the north, they had come.

This was the first mention Prisma had found of anything to do with the land north of Aobia, and she had practically scoured the first half of *The Book of Songs*. It was no small thing, either; the tome had the thickest spine she had ever seen on a single volume and pages thinner than anything she thought possible with Aobian parchment paper. She continued to leaf through.

Tala knew how important it was to find out more about the visitors and where they had come from. They were as tall as she and carried a similar sheen of silver hair. She let the mother press her hand to a cism, and the small thing responded with a burst of light like forks in a stormy sky. She decided these foreign Aobians must be protected at all costs and sought out for them a personal guard. Her advisors argued about the hidden agendas of the mother and son. Some believed they were sent to create fractures in Aobia, to challenge what they thought was true. Others thought they were visions, unreal and designed to toy with Tala's perception of reality. A few agreed that the mother and son were resources for the people of Aobia to learn about others like them, far away in distant lands, but their voices were suppressed by the opposition of their peers.

The day after Tala had given the mother and son a collective of guards, they were found dead in their quarters. Tala decided she had to go north and prove her advisors wrong. She would not let a claim for power divide her people, and nobody would dare touch her, the All-Mother.

At least, she wouldn't have thought so. Prisma dog-eared the page and closed the tome, thinking on what she knew of Tala. The female Aobian had rescued the original people from death in the Janub desert, finding succour in the Great Tree north of it. There had been other Great Trees around, too, supposedly. But within the past few centuries, nobody had seen them or any evidence of them, and *The Book of Songs* was amended to remove mentions of them. They shouldn't simply have vanished, but they had. Many, including herself, concluded that they hadn't been real, that they were instead falsities or assumptions that had been written about metaphorically.

But Tala had left her people and ventured north. It was the only time she had done so.

A rap of knuckles on the wooden door to her apartment sounded, and Prisma felt her heart drop. She rushed to the door and pulled it open, only for her sister Sleeper, Nischia, to barge in and embrace her.

"What is this mission?" Nischia whispered, her hot breath in Prisma's ear.

"I cannot say," Prisma gulped, tears rising with a lump in her throat. "But I'll be back. I don't know when, but I will." She said the words firmly but trailed off with as little confidence in them as she felt.

"How dare they?" Nischia exclaimed, pulling back and seizing her by the shoulders. "We just returned. The war was won. The people gone home. There must be *something* you can tell me." Her piercing blue eyes would not let Prisma hide the truth; Prisma knew Nischia as well as she'd come to know herself over the years. They had been bonded in trauma.

"If I speak," she croaked, "I break the promise I made to the Twelve."

Nischia groaned. "They toy with you, sister."

"They are the ones who govern Aobia," Prisma responded. "If they are toying with me, so be it. I must obey."

They stood opposite one another, like two armies on a battlefield. Silence moved between them until Nischia dropped her hands from Prisma's shoulders, sighing.

"What would you have me do, sister?" Prisma asked. "Be reasonable. Look for a Ghabbatian delivering falcon. They have white patches under their brown wings and long faces with short beaks. I'll write, every week. Maybe that way, you can stitch together fragments of the story as I go. But that is all I can promise."

"Will you take a *cism* with you?" Nischia asked. "We could bind them—"

"No," Prisma interrupted. "I shall not. If what I am seeking is to be found, I will not need one, anyway. Luminosity will, of course, subside in me over the course of my journey. I know the lack of it will exhaust me, but it must be done." Her justification was twofold, though she didn't say as much to Nischia. Firstly, the *cism* would be unnecessary if she was to encounter anything so great as Veil-Piercer. But secondly, if she did take a *cism* bound to her sister, she would give in to temptation and tell her everything, which was against orders from Koln, Loche, and the rest of the Twelve.

There had not been many times since she and Nischia had first met that she had seen her sister cry. But now, a quiet wellspring of tears ran down her cheeks, causing her silver hair to mat around her ears and neck. "I think it is time to say goodbye," she squeaked.

Prisma cupped Nischia's right hand in both of her own. "It is not forever, my sister. I will return as soon as I can."

Nischia nodded, sniffing back the tears. "I-I know. I love you." She moved back to the door and stepped out onto the precipice beyond the apartment.

"I love you too." The words seemed to last forever in the distance between them, and then Prisma pushed the door closed. She had to be the one to shut it.

NALOR

Late Autumn, 2055 AS

NALOR SCOWLED AT THE remains of the broken spear that filled the great wooden case upon his office desk. Talei sat in the chair opposite him, her leg jerking anxiously. The woman had barely survived the week prior and now here they were, back in the Presbytery of Dirt, focused on a new mission. He remembered his calling and forced himself to swallow the regret he felt at not having rescued the Kathani grindel in full. The shards of the broken blade known as Ka-Del were not enough to retrieve power from it; at least the Kathani man who had owned it couldn't do so, either. He had taken only one piece of metal from the spear before escaping the presbytery in Piat with his life.

The office where they now sat was nestled into the Presbytery of Dirt at the emperor's palace in Therador. They were stewing in the hot room, the woodfire flue in the adjoining hallway warming the place thoroughly. Talei wiped sweat from her brow, swallowing audibly.

"What is it?" Nalor asked.

"I cannot believe we lost Ka-Del," the woman hissed, turning her face away from him. "For years it was ours, and we let it go so easily."

"But you're happy your son survived, whether you say it so or not," he retorted, smirking. "He deserves to go back to the dirt." That Kathani snake, Jilo, and his weasel friends had ruined everything with his ridiculous plot for revenge.

"He is my son, just as you are!" Talei snapped. "What more could a mother want than for her son to live, even if he is her enemy?"

"The boundaries we live within are set for our continual improvement," Nalor replied. "It is good to limit passion in exchange for industriousness. We are only here to labour for the earth. I was not the one to construct these natural laws, but I will abide by them and reinforce them. This is the way of dirt."

"Humour me less," Talei murmured, crossing her arms. "What's next, anyway?"

"Our research is unending. If we can collect all these relics of the Aobian magic, we can find a way to master it." Nalor spun his quill in his hand before unrolling a new piece of parchment to lay out flat. He kept it pinned down on the table with the edge of his mask, which he wore with pride whenever he was in public. Thirteen years old that boy had been. He grinned to himself as he smoothed the paper out. He would never forget the day he'd made his first reclamation and put that child back where it belonged. Then, he'd caught a wild boar on his next hunt and fastened the tusks crudely to the forehead of the boy's skull. Now, it was the mark of his ordination into the Priesthood of Dirt.

How he wished he had put Talei's traitor son back where he belonged the night he'd come with the band of weasels to steal Ka-Del back from them. With the Kathani grindel destroyed, their sights would have to be set on greater things, a path he'd never thought he'd have to follow this soon. Grindels that were harder to obtain, partially rooted in an indistinguishable blend of history and myth. They'd known for years that Ka-Del was real after Talei had returned to the Empire from the riverside in the deep south.

He had already settled on the one he sought next. "Have you heard of Veil-Piercer?"

Talei's brows raised. "Surely you would not plan to find that? Therador has hunted it for centuries and never managed to prove whether it's even real."

"True enough. Veil-Piercer could be the greatest mark of power we've ever had. With it, the Emperor would be unstoppable. To channel the power of a remnant core with a single device would enable us to claim Q'ara without so much as a battle."

"A remnant core?"

"An Aobian who wielded Luminosity too carelessly, too fast. They burn out like a star, Mother. The light they produce is raw and destructive."

"It is a dangerous power you toy with, Nalor. Whose hands will command it, even if it is found? Is a Luminous object like that safe in the hands of any aside from the tree-dwellers?"

Nalor grimaced. Talei and her pessimism had gotten on his nerves over the past week. She usually had such a presence about her, an air of seniority. Despite knowing that, technically, she answered to him, he couldn't help but harbour some deep respect for his mother. But since losing Ka-Del, he felt as though he was stuck with a sombre child hidden in the body of a centuries-old crone.

"You test the dirt, woman," he spat. "We will find Veil-Piercer, and we will commandeer it. We have enough research to use. We know where to begin looking: far north, beyond the borders of Ghabbat."

"Our hubris grows too great for us to tame, Nalor," Talei said. "Pride is good in small doses. It's not the poison itself but the dose that will kill you. You know not what lies beyond those borders. Unsettled land, unexplored places, and the potential for disaster are all you are asking for."

"I see no hubris in actions I take out of necessity. And we, as an empire, *must* find these grindels." He stood, gesturing to the door. "I feel you have exhausted this conversation and my time. Please, be gone. I have plans to make."

Talei swept up her gown furiously and walked out, slamming the door behind her. The wafts of hot air from the flue blew towards Nalor, kicking his parchment up from the table. "Horrid bitch!" he snapped, smacking the paper back down.

Damn that woman, he thought. *Damn her to the dirt.*

Weeks went by, and Nalor took every second he could to study. Between, he attended his regular meditations and checked on Talei, who had grown wearier since the trip to Piat. Nalor had not been called to any other campaign for the war effort in Adira or the Mountain Pass to the south and watched from afar as criers came to the presbytery each week and gave the news.

The first two weeks were the same: no land had been conquered; Adira would not give up the fight. Then, the news grew more dire and Nalor began to suspect the Four-Front War was ending. Still, he kept his research up, combing through Aobian histories and stipends collected in the vast library at the presbytery.

The month after, Piat pulled out of the war effort, running low on resources. Sethiliquin was too remote, and they were no longer able to offer up more men or weaponry in a timely manner. Aobia and the Hidden Ones of the south had escalated their response at the mountain, and the Outfields of Adira were being held by Ghabbat and the enemy's northern militia.

Then the final blow struck and Nalor knew it was time to take charge and track down Veil-Piercer. The war was lost, and an armistice agreement was announced between the emperor and the Adiran king. Aobia and the Hidden Ones retreated, and the terms of their alliance with Adira were only made stronger by their promise to continue delivering clean water from the River Tomei's stretch beneath the Great Tree down to the coast.

Thankfully, with the war behind them, Nalor felt the urge to travel, and he had several promising texts marked for the task. The greatest of them, however, was an Aobian tome, *The Book of Songs*, a recount of histories told in verse or prose, some dating back to the moment the Aobians had escaped their perilous nomadic lifestyle in the Janub desert to settle in the first Great Tree and beyond. Hidden in the book were instances where the mechanics of Luminosity were explored on a level he'd never seen, but they weren't easy to decipher. Translations of the Old Tongue of Aobia were never entirely accurate. He knew translated copies existed, but this was the best he could have, for now.

It was the month after the armistice signing on the Mountain Pass, and Nalor had called together a team to go with him into the deep north. They would move through Ghabbat, beyond the mountains north of there, and track the great grindel. He met them in a conference room with a large stone table in the centre. On it was a long and extensive map of the north, reaching as far as any man had travelled. Beside it was paint, the Ichor of Dirt that high priests painted themselves with. He slathered it down his arms, around his neck, and up as high as his cheeks. When the people saw a high priest, they knew fear. You couldn't preach the importance of caring for the earth if you didn't inspire fear in the slothful masses.

The men he'd requested for the meeting slowly proceeded into the room and stood around the table as Nalor wiped his palms clean with a damp cloth. The other priests glared at him, waiting to receive their commands. Whether they wanted to be here or not did not matter. These men would work for the dirt, down to their very reclamation. But he knew, once he announced their objective, that the excitement would be contagious.

"Brothers in dirt," Nalor announced to the room, "it is time we played our strongest hand. Losing the Kathani grindel was a great blow and ending the Four-Front War an even greater one. But we will endure, for the dirt. We must continue, no matter the labour, no matter the challenge. Remember, men, that you are dirt."

"And to the dirt we must return," the priests murmured back. This was a tight team of four of Nalor's most trusted companions in the priesthood. The youngest recruit, and most recently ordained, Kai the Bold, spoke first.

"What is our mission, brother?" he asked. He looked no more than a boy, but his wisdom was contained in multitudes beyond his years.

Nalor grinned. "We go to the deep north, beyond the Ghabbatian borders. As the Kathani grindel has been lost, we must be efficient. I hope to return within two months, no more. We cannot prolong the Bloodline's dreams."

"Assuredly," replied Veis the Firm. He had just returned from his emissary trip to Adira with the prince, Jurin, but he was ready. He was always ready, and that was what Nalor loved about him. Veis was frequently away, but when he returned, he took orders and left just as quickly.

"Be attentive to the plan," Nalor went on. "I have drafted it, and we can modify it as necessary. He pointed to the parchment he'd weighed down on the table. "This is a rough rendition of the terrain we are envisioning lies beyond Ghabbat's mountains."

On the parchment was a carefully drawn map postulating the kind of land they might encounter beyond the northern ranges. No man, at least no Theradoran man, had ever gone further north. But there were historical reports and stories that drew a consistent enough picture of what might lie there. Old tales of strange creatures and trees akin to the Great Tree of Aobia, all the way to the south.

"The mountains of Ghabbat, as we know, are frigid compared to our own," Nalor said. "Prepare accordingly. We will move quickly and ration. The hunt may be necessary for survival, but we will try to oversupply in Ghabbat first. Reclaim what life you can, as it is what we owe to the dirt for our own."

Scalmer the Wulf grunted, wrapping his furs around his shoulders tightly as if already feeling the Ghabbatian cold. He was the priest who had taken the Kathani grindel Ka-Del years before. He was old now—so old that there was no reasonable explanation for why he appeared half his age. He wore the stamp of the deer upon his chest, though his mask was a fusion of wolf and boar, two kills he had made by hand, or so the tale went. "Whatever meatlife we kill falls into our merciful hunt at the hands of providence, and providence alone, brother."

"Assuredly," Nalor said. "Despite this, we must be prepared to go days without encountering meatlife. There is not much that can live so high in those ranges."

They nodded. Here in Therador, they worked for their meatlife, the centre of their meals, through ministry and reclamation. But out in the world, they had to maintain the rigour of work in other ways. They would hunt and survive.

Nalor knew they could do this. These were the most fierce and relentless priests he knew. They would stop at nothing, even their own reclamations, to further the progression of Therador's force. This continent belonged to those who were strong enough to take it by the horns and contain it; just because the war had come to an end, it didn't mean they would stop trying.

They needed these grindels. To unlock the power of Luminosity through the collective force of all magical objects was a dream centuries in the making. They were close to making it a reality. No more imbalance of powers between the Aobian Sleepers and everyone else. To heal the sick, power machinery, and maybe even raise the dead were just some of the benefits of the Aobian gift of light. If Therador led the distribution of Luminosity, they'd control Q'ara under the guise of a level playing field.

"After the mountains, what should we anticipate?" Sachil the Fierce was a menacing figure, standing taller than the rest of the bunch. He had an angular, chiselled look to him and shoulders broader than the trunk of the Aobian Great Tree. Despite his brawn, however, he liked to plan ahead, and Nalor knew the ambiguity of the north would be his greatest obstacle to overcome yet.

But this man came from a long generation of battlers, and he carried every scar. These days, he commandeered the paid mercenary group, the Nightingales, to scour the land for any Luminous artifacts or clues as to their whereabouts. Being in charge of a band of thieves with uncertain loyalties was a step in the right direction.

"I don't know," Nalor said. "The map ends at the mountains of Ghabbat. But I'm willing to vouch for our success on the principle alone. We are capable, brothers. We are powerful. We've faced death before, and we'll face it again, lest we go back to the dirt." The room carried a mixture of nods, grunts, and wobbly silence. "We leave at first light for Ghabbat on horseback. Be ready and ensure anything you're working on in the city is taken over by someone equally equipped. Talei comes with us. Her guidance and expertise in grindel research are needed. She doesn't know it yet, so have your wits about you. The mood she'll be in when she's put on horseback at dawn will be enough to kill us all before we even set off."

The men chuckled as they started to leave the room, but Nalor cleared his throat to get their attention one last time. "One last thing, brothers. If any of us go back to the dirt, it will be in honour, not despair. Is that understood?"

The men cast their eyes away from one another, and Nalor knew they got the message. It would be easy, depending on the circumstances, to give up. But he could not be the one to condemn his own brothers. He *would* do it, however, if it meant his own life, and the work he'd done with it, hung in the balance.

PRISMA

Early Autumn, 2055 AS

ONLY TALA'S DAUGHTERS PRODUCED children, and they did so with a select few people who could not Sleep. This was the natural process for the All-Mother's rule to continue in Aobia.

Prisma sighed as she turned on her bed, closing *The Book of Songs*. If ever there was an explanation good enough to justify why Sleepers lived a life of abstinence, it was probably this. And it didn't really tell her anything.

She had to leave tomorrow, and yet there was something she still needed to do, though her mind continually warned her against it. She rolled off the bed and gently fluffed her hair, pushing out the flatter sides into their regular curls from where her head had been on the pillow.

She left, quiet as a chippermouse, and stepped lightly down the stairs of her apartment building in the Mind to the rear garden entrance. Then, she moved briskly through the ornately trimmed hedgerows and wooden, branchrendered benches until she reached a tiny gate that let her out to the wide branchroad that ran through the Mind, the district of the Sleepers. A lonely cabriolet sat parked on the other side, its attached horse braying with impatience.

Before she approached, she carefully retrieved an imbued *cism* from her navy-blue cloak. Light sat within it like still liquid. The tiny glass sphere was a way for her to store and use Luminosity away from her Orb, which reimbursed her with Sleep. She pressed her hands to the globe and felt Luminosity cling to her from within as the light leapt to life. Around her, the sounds of the world dimmed. She was shielded now and could speak freely without risking another Sleeper being alerted to her active mind in the middle of the night. She walked across the road to the cab.

"Parkins." She nodded to the horse, who considered her wearily.

"You greet the horse before me, my lady?" an older Aobian said from the driver's seat. Frenet was a speedy driver who was largely responsible for escorting both Prisma and Loche, together or separately, around the Great Tree for business. He was mostly a loyal driver, too, and respected the Sleepers enough for Prisma to know that she could trust him to keep quiet about what she was to do this night and those that had come before.

"You know I can count on you, Frenet," she winked as she hopped into the seat beside him.

"Ever the playful one, Lady Prisma. Come, Parkins, we can't be here all night!" Frenet grinned as he urged the horse into motion with a gentle tug of the reins. "I remember the first time you sat next to me on the driver's bench. I thought your superior was about to faint in the back."

"We are no different, you and I," she reminded him. "Your station should not be considered any lower than mine." She stuck by that mantra. Throughout her life, she'd learned that she was, by definition, revered by many of the common folk throughout Aobia. But for what she saw it as, it was merely a facade. She hadn't picked this life, this blessing … it had picked her.

"You're a brave soul, Lady Prisma," Frenet said, quieter now. "And I hope you are granted the farewell you deserve, with no ill consequences."

"If there are any, they won't come from him," Prisma said. No, it would come from Loche, and the others of the Twelve, and it could mark the end of her place in the Magisterium if she wasn't careful. She would never understand the meaning of remaining celibate. What cause did love have in the unmaking of a Sleeper? It seemed the answer lay with the outdated traditions of Tala, the first All-Mother, and the message written in *The Book of Songs*.

The time passed with Frenet in silence until they reached the home of the one Prisma loved. "Where are they sending you, Lady Prisma?" Frenet asked.

"I cannot say, sadly. I'd tell you if I hadn't first been asked not to," she said somberly, before reaching across the bench to give

Frenet a quick hug. "Please say you'll be my driver when I get home."

"Is that a proposal?" Frenet said with a chuckle. Prisma tried to respond but only a waning half smile emerged. "Well, I wouldn't want anything else, my lady," Frenet said. "Now, go tell him you love him and the child. Do you want me to wait?"

Prisma shook her head. "I'll call another cab with the rising sun. I wouldn't want you being caught up in this mess." And it *was* a mess. She smiled one last time at Frenet before taking her hand off her *cism*. The light swirling around inside dimmed instantly and the ambient sounds of the world around them—leaves rustling, birds quietly flapping their wings overhead—returned.

She waved a morose goodbye to Frenet as she approached the neatly kept branchrendered home that belonged to her heart, a magisterial cleric named Altaea, whom she had met several years ago working for Loche, her superior. And it *had* been years; years of stepping back and forth with Altaea, either giving him too much affection or shutting herself off like a valve. She had also learned to hide what she shared with him from everyone else around her for their protection. She was a Sleeper, and not only was the concept of romance unbecoming, it was also folly. Romantic love was a threat to the industriousness of a Sleeper's role in shaping and protecting the people of Aobia. In the first year she'd gotten to know Alt, she'd also wrestled with the dilemma. Unspeakable guilt still continued to fall on her.

Two years ago, in the midst of the ever-growing Four-Front War, everything with Alt had changed. Prisma had borne a child.

It had nearly broken her to know that she had broken all the commands given to her with her Blessing to be Sleeper. But she'd known, when the child had come, that she was to protect it at all costs. With everything she had.

From a distance.

Their daughter had been born healthy and happy within the walls of Alt's quiet home, tucked at the end of a limb of the Tree. Prisma clutched the trauma of the night with the same visceral intermingling of emotions that had set her on her path to being a Sleeper all those years ago when she'd survived the Fever. Every week thereafter, for the past two years, Prisma had engaged in Sleep in her Orb in smaller amounts than usual, to be able to watch and intercept any Sleeper poking around Altaea. Clerics were audited regularly by the Magisterium to maintain compliance and trustworthiness, but Alt had not once been touched. Sure enough, when Prisma left the Tree to go to war at the Mountain Pass, the feeling that Ti might be discovered clawed at her continually. Relief had overcome her when she'd gotten home. Now, she was to be gone again.

Something interesting had happened during her time at war, however: her Orb had moved. A Sleeper's Orb was said to be the spectral incarnation of their hearts. It went where it was supposed to and stayed with the Sleeper all their life. For the past year or so, hers had led her back to Alt, her beloved, and her precious child. It had danced between there and the battlefield when she'd been away. It protected them all. Now their forbidden love, and their family, would be snuffed out like an emptied Luminous lamp.

Turned off, never to be relit, unless a Sleeper imbued it once more.

Unless she could make her way home again, this was to be the end.

The door creaked as it opened out to the night. He hadn't been asleep. Altaea stood before her, dark rings beneath his eyes, silver hair messily tied back. Of course, she knew he was already tired and that this moment would devastate him, perhaps hurt him more than it hurt her. She leapt into his open arms.

"Heart of mine, we have been going mad without you," he cooed into her ear. "Tiun could not sleep." She felt goosebumps ride her arms. And then, she started to cry, and Altaea pulled her even more tightly against him. "What is it, my love?"

She had to say it. She *had* to tell him. It was now or never. She swallowed and looked him in the eyes, unsure of whether the truth would come out of her mouth.

"I have to Sleep, Alt," she said. "I am worn thin, unimbued. That is all it is. It makes me more emotional than normal." She gave him an uneasy smile, weighed down by her half truth.

Altaea held her out from him and studied her carefully. She held her eyes open with false confidence, knowing it wouldn't convince him.

"I understand," he eventually said. "It is important. The little one is asleep now. I can listen for her tonight. You do what you must." He had folded. He knew that in this dance with Prisma, he never had the leading foot. Everything that had led them here, now, was a result of his concessions, his need to fold for her. If he did not, he risked their relationship being discovered. As a cleric of one of the Twelve, Altaea could be imprisoned and prosecuted. Prisma could be exiled. The child … gods forbid anything should happen to the child.

Too much hinged on their discretion. Somehow, Alt was always able to shut off his passion like a faucet right before the sink spilled over. It astonished her, and yet even though she needed him to do it, she couldn't help but feel slighted every time he did so. He could not cry her name from the branches of Aobia. He could not court her for marriage. And yet, he had no choice but to cling on to her like an addict to crispwater.

He could not live one day as though the next was guaranteed. It tore Prisma apart. Perhaps leaving for the north was the best thing she could do by him. Perhaps he could finally have his life and find love like he deserved.

She regarded him for one final moment, reaching out to stroke his cheek. A sad smile lingered on his lips, and finally, she swept past him, past the closed door Tiun slept behind, and into the back of the home. She hesitated.

Then she turned back and opened the door quietly. In her cot, Tiun looked like a reflection of the stars in the sky. Golden locks mixed with the silver that she would grow into crowned her head, and her sweet, sleeping face glistened like fine porcelain.

"My heart," Prisma whispered and leant down to stroke her precious cheek. Then, she left the room, ignoring the urge to run back in and pick up her daughter, the tiny creature nobody knew about. She closed the door, guilt pulling at her like a tightening noose. *You are the one letting this happen. Only you.*

Tucked behind a square annex of bookcases was Prisma's thrumming Orb, its space-filling orange hue calling to her with the same whirring song she'd heard since they first became aware of one another. Since the day of her Blessing, when the Fever broke. This was to be the last time she would Sleep to be imbued with Luminosity before she departed Aobia, unless of course, the Orb went with her. She hoped it didn't, for Alt's sake. She could take no risks. It was a risk enough that her Luminosity would run out during her travel north.

It was also the last time she would see her secret family, perhaps forever. It tore her apart that she could not tell him, but it was for the best. He deserved to be free, to never need to hide such a large part of his life from others. His own parents and siblings lived without knowledge that he and Prisma had been together for so long—they didn't even know Tiun existed. The shame wouldn't just break him. It would pit him against the laws he vouched for in his own work for the Magisterium.

You can turn around and put your arms around him one last time, she thought. The thrum of the Orb grew louder, rising in her ears and swallowing the other sounds of the world around her: her footsteps on the wooden floor, the sound of Altaea moving around in the kitchen. She'd grown strong at refusing the Orb's song when faced with it, because she had gotten into the habit of Sleeping so often to shield Alt and the baby. But tonight, she *needed* the Sleep. Without it, she'd be leaving Aobia naked and powerless. The fear of that alone moved her feet into the edges of the warm light.

The Orb subsumed her, body and soul, and she began her restless Sleep. *Goodbye, my loves,* she thought as her mind let go.

When morning came, something awakened Prisma's senses. She couldn't explain how, but she knew it was time to leave. Her sister Nischia never enjoyed the same control and always had to fight to escape Sleep. But for Prisma, it felt natural to climb out of the Orb and know that new light travelled through her veins.

She tiptoed to the front door, passing Altaea's bedroom along the way. He was sound asleep. The baby would be too, and Prisma knew this was her only chance to leave without disturbing her.

No goodbyes are worth the breaking of two hearts, she concluded. She sucked in a breath at the prospect of collecting her things and leaving Aobia. It always felt unnatural, the first time she placed her feet on the forest floor. Of course, workers at the River Tomei experienced this on a daily basis, but it wasn't the same as stepping outside of the shade of Aobia's Great Canopies.

When Prisma had finally caught two different cabs back to her home, she arrived to the familiar face of Loche, who was waiting on the steps of the apartment building. "It is time, Prisma," Loche said, the creases in the corners of his eyes stretching into a painful smile. Even *he* was feeling morose about her departure, her unblinking superior who had never once showed an ounce of fear when she'd been sent to fight on the front at the Mountain Pass. What was to befall her on this journey?

"I'll gather my things," she croaked, walking past him and into the building.

"Wait," Loche called to her from behind. She turned, dreading what he would say next. *Where were you so early in the morning? What were you doing?*

"If I don't get a second to say this later, child," he began, "know that I am proud of you. Of everything you've become. I … know I haven't always had the biggest heart out of the two of us. My stoicism can be stifling."

"Stoicism?" Prisma said with a cheeky grin.

Loche chuckled. "I suppose I am simply saying … you mean more to me than I could ever put into words."

A mixture of relief and joy caused her to practically run at him, and when he caught her with a loud "Oomph!" the world disappeared. Just for a moment, it was her in the arms of her mentor and nothing else mattered.

"Well, on with it, then," Loche finally said, gently letting her go. "Gather your things and meet me at the service elevator."

NALOR

Late Autumn, 2055 AS

I T HAD BEEN A week since the party had left Therador, and they had finally reached the city-state of Ghabbat. After the city, there would be nothing but the great beyond: no towns or villages. Not only that, but there was no place they were welcome. Nalor supposed it was for good reason. Ghabbat would be the most hostile, however, as these hill people were in an alliance with Adira, Therador's enemies in the Four-Front War. It didn't matter that armistice had taken place. These people would carry the scars of the war with them for years to come, and Therador would always be the target.

The group's supplies were dwindling now, and Ghabbat was the only option they had to stock up before they faced the unknown. Nalor could only hope that while they were there, they'd simply have to deal with sour looks rather than a riot.

Ghabbat was built into the highlands of Northern Q'ara, against a backdrop of alpine forestry that rose into dark grey mountains that touched the sky. It was no mistake that the Ghabbatians were quiet in their ways and meddled little in the business of Q'aran politics. They lived under a damned shadow.

Now, it was noon as Nalor and his crew moved through the streets, and the sun was only just out over the city. He'd instructed the men to keep their masks strapped to the front of their packs instead of their faces, so as to avoid whispers around the city. Despite this, people were talking, some even hiding behind pillars or going inside buildings as the leather-clad Theradoran men walked along the streets, pewter-inlaid steel spears in hand.

They were hunting for a finer tavern, the kind with a bath, as it was the only luxury Nalor thought would afford him the right to speak with Talei, who had remained silent as a mute since they'd embarked on their journey from Therador. She was not happy that his ambitions drove him to Veil-Piercer. But he needed her, not in the same way he had as a boy, perhaps, but enough to put up with her mood.

"Excuse me," he said in broken Ghabbatian to a nearby local who was walking a donkey down the opposite side of the street. "Do you know the best tavern in town? We are travellers, and we have come a long way."

The bald, olive-skinned man shrugged. "You hail from the Empire, am I correct?"

Nalor shuffled on his feet as the man's donkey brayed. "Uh, yes, you are correct."

"Well, then," the man said, "there's only one place that will work. Pomegranates & Tears on the southern edge of the city. You're lucky you haven't stirred up worse." He nodded at Nalor as he led his donkey away through the crowds and disappeared.

The only one that would work? Nalor looked back at his crew and Talei. They were exhausted. He didn't have time to figure out what that man had meant. "Pomegranates & Tears," he said as he walked back over to his men. "Southern edge of the city. We must've already passed it."

"Dirt," Scalmer snorted. "Let's get there then. We can't take any more of your mother's silence. Give her what she needs and restock our supplies. Then we can be on the move again."

"Right," Nalor replied, gritting his teeth. Scalmer wasn't one to be toyed with. Nalor needed his men on his side, and this was the first bite from one of them that he'd received since they'd left Therador.

They came to the tavern in question, adorned with several windows that had been painted black on the inside, some broken stones on the ground that had once filled the roughly hewn walls, and a sign that made him wince. Where it had once said 'Pomegranates & Tears', it now said 'Theradoran Tears'.

"Wonderful," Nalor said as he pushed the brittle timber door open.

The inside smelled like an incensed morgue with dirty, leather-skinned folk smoking crude black stuff out of long clay pipes and sucking back pitchers of what looked like grit-filled mud water. At the bar stood a tall woman with wiry grey hair and sunken black eyes. She looked like she'd had enough of it all for longer than Nalor had been alive.

"Travellers, are ye?" she said with barely a greeting. When she half smiled, Nalor saw the tremendous space in her mouth where several teeth had once been.

"You are correct, ma'am. We need a place to stay."

The woman stifled a cackle. "A place to play?" She kept on laughing with her mouth closed so the odd sound bounced around between her cheeks in a muted way. Finally, she spoke in clear Theradoran. "You don't know your Ghabbatian well, do you, enemy priest?"

Nalor sighed as the men behind him chuckled. Talei, however, remained demure. "Just get us a couple of rooms for the next two nights. We can bunk. We're not precious. We aren't here to start anything."

"That what ye do over in Therador, eh? Bunk with your brothers?" The woman giggled.

"Where do you come from, ma'am?" Nalor demanded. "Because if you're one of ours, we can have your labour assessed."

He watched the darkness bloom in her eyes, and she hesitated before answering. "Not one of yours, thank the Sea."

"You're Adiran then." He said it smugly. Of course they were here, in a hostel that contained people barely hanging on to their dear lives, who were all politically opposed to the Empire, right after the most tumultuous war of the past century. Nalor should've realised that man was sending them to a place like this. They didn't have the same power here as they did in Therador.

They were in the northernmost city on Q'ara, which was in a centuries-old alliance with the Sea Kingdom, Adira. He had to assume everyone hated them.

"Tell me, woman," Nalor sneered. "Why is this the only place that we should stay in?"

"We don't want Priests of Dirt in our city, whether a peace agreement has been struck or not," the woman sneered. "But I'll take ye in if it means some coin to get by. I'm likely the only one that would do so. Rest of them would want ye dead. All of ye. In exchange for the blood you've let from our loved ones and the blood you'll continue to let."

Just then, the door of the tavern flew open, its wobbly knob splitting the timber as it struck the entry wall. A haggard young woman puffed and panted, keeling over against the doorframe. She should've been red from being so out of breath, but instead, she was ghost white.

She stumbled forward, collapsing over the top of a table where some grim-looking men were smoking. She knocked ash all over the place before striking the ground. "Another drunk?" Sachil asked. "What kind of place is this, anyway?"

The woman was out cold, and people were beginning to crowd around her. Nalor pushed through them, watching the young person intently. What had happened, he'd barely begun to take in, but—

She rose, her neck craning upwards as though her body weighed no more than a flower petal on the breeze. Her hair was oddly grey for one so young, a strange sheen of silver on parts of it, nearly illuminated. Her eyes were open, but there was … Nalor shivered. *Nothing there. No pupils, no colour.* What had happened to this woman?

She fell back again, but one of the smoking men caught her head before it hit the stone. The people in the room were an odd mixture of Adiran, with their olive skin and fairer hair; Ghabbatian, with their even darker tone and black, curly waves; and Sethi, the strange, angular-faced people of the mountains to the far west of Therador. At that moment, however, they seemed taken aback by the Theradoran priests, maskless though they were, standing around the random woman.

"Let us see her," Nalor said, snapping into motion. He gestured for the men to move aside, but they stayed with the woman, cradling her neck and shaking their heads. "We can help," Nalor insisted, setting his long spear onto the table beside him.

Reluctantly, those in the room made space for Nalor and the others to step closer, and he started checking the woman over. A hand to her neck told him she was breathing, but an ear above her mouth told him it was not deeply. Not nearly enough to keep her alive. "Kai, I need you to …"

He didn't have to finish the sentence before young Kai began to pump his fists against her chest. He heard the snap and crackle of ribs and winced. Still, her heartbeat was dwindling. Kai knew what to do; he was one of the most medically proficient out of all their brothers in the priesthood.

Talei was at their side in an instant, cold washcloth at the ready. She pressed the cloth to the woman's forehead and held it there as Kai kept pumping. Nalor felt his heart race as hers slowed beneath his fingers. Who was this woman? She was oddly tall, long-limbed, and as young as she looked mature. She was unlike any person he'd ever seen.

Before that could be answered, however, she gasped, sucking in what seemed like an eternal breath before lurching upright. Her eyes rolled back, and an inhuman voice left her lips, like the sound of a thousand layered screams.

"THE EYES!" the young woman screamed. "THE EYES ARE UPON US ALL!"

The light seemed to vanish from inside the room. Darkness settled like a sheet, dropped onto them all from above. Nalor's skin crawled, the hair on his arms standing up. The silence in the room screamed for attention.

Out of the darkness, light exploded, light as bright as the centre of the sun. Nalor shielded his eyes as he heard people crying out. It dimmed, slowly, enough that he could see it was emanating from the woman, like fire beneath her skin.

The woman finally slumped over, blood pouring from her mouth, her nose, her ears and eyes. Blood poured like a river, filling the cloth Talei abandoned and covering Nalor's sleeves and pants. So much blood soaked the floor and the woman, so that she looked more like a clot than a body. The place grew darker once more, until her blood stopped flowing and Nalor's breath caught.

She was well and truly dead.

PRISMA

Autumn's Heart, 2055 AS

FLOCKS OF BIRDS SOARED over the mountains of Ghabbat as Prisma woke up surrounded by their heights. Four weeks had passed since she had left Aobia, and she was finally feeling normal, though she was surrounded by the earth that belonged to the humans rather than the wood of the Great Tree.

Cold air had become colder up on the slopes. Gluggy, melted bits of snow struggled to linger on the rocky ground, but that was a sure sign that a more brutal frost was ahead. Prisma had been crossing this terrain for days now and was starting to run out of food. In some ways, she wasn't complaining; there was only so much a diet of Ghabbatian ration food—flatbread, raisins, and dried cheese—could do to make up for the fresh fruits, nuts, and vegetables she ate regularly back in Aobia. But she had to be a realist: this was all she had left. She looked down, demure, at the scattered crumbs, raisins, and flakes of cheese in her hand and shoved it all down her throat in a single wolfish gulp.

Prisma looked over at the scattered branches and twigs that the wind had blasted out of the pine trees the night before. Part of her wanted nothing more than to use her Luminosity to start a fire and then warm herself beside it, study, and move on with fresh, rested blood running through her veins. But fire was the antithesis of life and despite her distance from home, she wondered if anybody would know if she broke such an important Aobian custom.

She sighed, looking at the book that lay partially wrapped in the thick fleece bedroll she had purchased in Ghabbat. *The Book of Songs* had revealed things that, in the last few desperate days, had urged her to press on. The greatest of those was the implication that a Great Tree beyond Ghabbat was not only real but had actually been seen and reported on by Tala, the first All-Mother. Depending on how one might view their faith in Aobian history and tradition, this was either celebratory news or evidence that the modern myth of the north had been perpetuated through a vital text of the Aobian people.

I wish I knew what to believe, she thought while she rolled up her pack and filled it with her few possessions, including the book. As she wound it up one final time, however, her hand slipped, and the bedroll came loose, dropping her things and *The Book of Songs* face down in the snow.

"Roots below!" she swore, gathering it up and wiping the wet slosh from the pages that had fallen open. Unfortunately, the thin parchment meant the words were nearly indecipherable with the stain of water on them, and she let out a cry of frustration. Her hands were so cold, she couldn't even turn the pages to dry them off. Nearby, a flat-topped stone jutted out of the ground and she moved to sit there, holding the book out under the sunlight.

The words, smeared as they were, set in the sunlight well enough, and she read the pages as she waited for them to dry. *Tala taught the Sleepers how to create and, equally, to destroy by using Luminosity. Imbuing an object did not just fill it with light. It also allowed the Sleeper to attribute rules, meanings, and other conditions. Binding two* cism *together, for example, allowed people to communicate over long distances. Similarly, oathstones, though requiring a substantial effort to create, were given when one Sleeper owed another a debt of some kind: until the debt was given, the oathstone could not be removed from the wearer. It was an honour device, and ...*

The words following on were smudged badly, but Prisma felt her eyebrows lift with intrigue. She'd never heard any other Sleeper mention an oathstone. What was it? She quickly turned the pages, but the topic had already changed. Scowling, Prisma went back and reread the same, unsmudged words: *... until the debt was given, the oathstone could not be removed from the wearer.*

An idea struck her as she pulled out her journal to add a note about the oathstones. Book under arm, she furiously scribbled down the basics of the oathstone with a gold-adorned quill Altaea had given to her. Then she closed the journal and stood, breathing deeply.

She had to go, to find something that indicated another Tree's existence, and *soon.* The Luminosity she'd Slept for in Aobia was running out, as she had needed to draw on it for light, to read and see in the dark. She had no *cism* filled or ready to wield, which was an affronting fact. If she ran out, she'd feel naked and more lost than ever.

But if I can get there, she thought with her teeth gritted in determination, *I can try to craft one of these stones and force it upon Veil-Piercer.* It was a crazy idea, she knew, but it could mean the difference between certain death and being able to retrieve Veil-Piercer for further study in Aobia.

Prisma continued to plod along through the snow for what became hours. Still, she was going mostly downhill after cresting a nearby mountaintop earlier. Her thoughts went with her the entire way, distracting her from the harshness of the elements and the strenuousness of the walking. She passed a bush riddled with air-dried remnants of what must have been mulberries once and ate them sparingly while she took in the environment around her. Aside from the slopes before her, everything was coated in white. It seemed even the sun was, blending into the blue that was painted around it. Until she'd see bits of green poking through the snow, she knew she was nowhere near the rough region where the 'lost' Tree was said to have been.

Prisma promptly ran out of breath and found a fallen log to sit upon. The sound of flapping wings sounded overhead. She grinned, looking up to see a brown, Ghabbatian falcon with a wingspan nearly the width of her arms. A low coo sounded from it, a word of greeting. "Tayriah," she called. "You have returned to me. How is my sister?"

Around the neck of the delivery bird she had purchased in Ghabbat was a ribbon containing two small scrolls of parchment. Nischia had written to her, judging by the handwriting on one. But so had *someone else*. The letter was unaddressed. Her throat became dry and her hands clammy as she quickly unfastened the ribbon from Tayriah. Was it, somehow, a letter from *Altaea*?

She couldn't imagine what Altaea had thought of her leaving, couldn't entertain the thought of him realising she was gone. It had been so unfair. And Tiun … just the thought of her child brought her to tears. Altaea had stood by her like a post in steady soil, yet the punishment of their forbidden love—and worse, their forbidden family—fell upon him. This was what he got in exchange for the love of a Sleeper. Abandonment.

"I cannot," she said, the words coming out between a throaty breath. "What kind of mother am I?" Tayriah cocked her head at Prisma, her swirling blue eyes curious. Or, maybe, encouraging. *Come,* she seemed to say to Prisma with another whistling coo. *Open it.*

Prisma gripped one note and pulled it open, teeth gritted. It was from Nischia. She looked at the falcon, who gazed back at her with the same forlorn stare. "There is something odd about your eyes," she murmured to the bird. "Your keeper told me as much. Falcons have wells for eyes, and yet yours look like the sky or the stars contained in it." The bird, of course, did nothing so much as poke its head deep into the snow suddenly, retrieving a small mountain shrew and gobbling it down. Prisma returned to Nischia's missive.

Sister, it read. *I long to see you. Your carrier bird seemed to know my ache and bade me quicken my writing, as though it needed to get back to tell you just that. Please come home, with all your limbs and wits about you. N.*

Prisma snickered at the brief note and let her sad eyes wander back over to the other scroll. She sucked in a breath, readying herself to read it. *No,* she thought, standing. Tayriah flew up to a nearby branch, ready. "I cannot, Tayriah. We must keep going. You can stay with me tonight and then tomorrow, you should leave for the Tree." A thought struck her. "How did you know to visit Altaea?" she asked. The bird looked back at her, this time with an empty expression. It didn't have the answer. It was just a bird. An impressive bird maybe, but a bird, nonetheless.

"Let us carry on, then." Hope filled her that maybe the second letter was a follow-up message from Nischia or something from Loche. Perhaps Nischia had spoken to Loche, and—

She wouldn't have, though. She was not meant to correspond with Prisma, and that was that.

Prisma stalked through the trees for the next hour, pausing to scoop up small mouthfuls of fresh snow. Tayriah flew high overhead, staying with her the entire way. Eventually, the slope she had been heading down scooped back up steeply before her. She could try to circumvent it, but if she made it to the top of the thin spire, maybe it would give her an impression of the land on the other side of the mountain ranges.

Above her, Tayriah cawed and began to circle. It was not prey she saw; if it was, she would circle silently.

As Prisma scaled the ever-steep mountainside, finally needing to grab onto tree limbs or large, jutting stones, she found herself sweating profusely despite the bitterly cold air. Time seemed to drag, but eventually, she hauled her weight up a final outcropping of rock, pausing for a few breaths before heading across the narrow ridge at the peak. The mist from earlier in the day had gone and she let her jaw drop as she took in the sights. The view was breathtaking, the river running through the heart of the mountain and down into the woods on the other side. Tayriah cawed again and Prisma chuckled in delight at the awe. Then, she turned her head to the left, in the direction of the distant ocean, and there it was.

"Never in my wildest dreams ..." she uttered.

Before her stood a staggeringly tall Great Tree, different in its structure, its limbs, and its canopy to the one back home. It sat like a staff of the gods in the middle of the river, causing the water to fork off in two directions; one end ran right into a lake at the base of a nearby mountain. The pine trees that dotted the landscape of the Ghabbatian mountains looked like miniatures in comparison to this new Great Tree. Tayriah flapped down to her, resting her piercing claws on Prisma's shoulder and dousing her in shadow.

"Tala said the Tree was standing like a divider between the forks of a river," Prisma whispered to the bird. "That's all I need to find. Then I can go home." She pulled out her roll of parchment paper and tore off two pieces, writing her messages onto each, before folding them up and wrapping them with separate threads. Tayriah dropped to the ground so that Nischia could tie the ribbon around the grand bird's neck.

"You know your duty," she said to Tayriah, who cooed in response. "Don't get eaten by any Greatbirds, you hear me?" she said half-jokingly. The bird took to the sky without another sound but the enormous, sweeping wind that was created by the flaps of her wings.

"I'm here," Prisma said. "I found it."

NALOR

Late Autumn, 2055 AS

NALOR LAY SLEEPLESS AS the rest of the men and his mother slept in the bunks below him. He looked up at the patchy, smoke-stained roof, both arms tucked beneath his head. They couldn't save that woman. Afterwards, while Nalor and the crew purchased new clothes to replace the stained ones, the Ghabbatian men took her away in a cart covered with hessian to be burned, for fear her mind had been overtaken by demons. Nalor, however, had a feeling in the pit of his stomach that that wasn't what had happened.

He shook his head. They didn't have time for this. They would move on from enemy territory the next day and continue into the deep north. He would not stop until they retrieved Veil-Piercer. It was everything that Therador hinged on. With it accessible to the Empire, they'd never feel the need to surrender again, no matter how great the pressure the Adiran alliance put on them.

Sure, Nalor was aware of the emperor's tyrant inclinations, and he knew well that the grindels were only being sourced to seek out continental power. But as a Priest of Dirt, the journey he'd endured to find the grindels was more than that. Humans needed to work hard. It was their calling to labour in exchange for their fleeting lives. So, if he had been born into a system whereby he must follow the emperor's orders, follow them he would. Why would he risk his soul otherwise?

Suddenly, a *tap, tap, tap* against the window roused him from his thoughts. He propped himself up on his elbows and the bed creaked, causing Sachil, who was on the bunk below, to start snoring. *Dirt*, Nalor swore internally. He rocked back and forth, causing the whole bed frame to move, and Sachil rolled over, the snoring ceasing.

Nalor plonked his head back on the pillow. It seemed that none of the forces of the night wished for him to sleep.

"Thank you," came a wispy voice, and Nalor sucked in a breath, aghast. Before him hung the hollow, nearly transparent visage of a woman, the one who had died in the tavern earlier that afternoon.

Nalor let out a short cry and shoved himself upright. "What … ?" Goosebumps perked up along his arms.

"You fear me, and yet you walk the streets with the skulls of the dead wrapped around your face?"

"Wh-who are you?" Nalor stuttered.

"Do you not know me?" The ghost sidled up to him, kneeling on the end of the bunk. *Can a ghost kneel?* he thought.

"You and your friends tried to save me today but I am glad that you failed. I am bound by debt to you because now, I am free. Free of the eyes."

The eyes. The woman had screamed about those in her final breaths. "You thank me for freeing you?" Nalor asked.

The ghost seemed to shimmer like a reflection on a dark lake, the wisps of her once-silver hair catching the moonlight through the window. "I will thank you for failing to save me, until the day this fleeting form of mine is gone forever." She said it in such an ominous manner, Nalor felt his skin crawl.

"What are they? The eyes?" Nalor insisted. In the hours since her death, he'd wondered whether the woman had been some kind of crispwater addict who had overdosed beyond the point of comprehension. He'd thought, perhaps wrongly, that she had been just another instance of wasted potential. Another person to be reclaimed by the dirt.

"The eyes ..." The woman's words trailed off as she turned her head, looking out the window opposite Nalor. She sat there, silent as death, for a long while before answering. "The eyes are many, not one. They belong to a creature. They were watching me. *All the time.*"

"A creature?" Nalor asked.

The spirit nodded. "A ... perversion. Fuelled with the impurest light. Made up of many broken souls. And they will overwhelm all of you if you do not stay away."

Nalor frowned. "Stay away from where?"

The spirit looked confused. "I can … take you there?"

Nalor thought for a moment. This spirit knew something he didn't. If the creature she spoke of was hidden north of the city, he'd take whatever advantage he could get. Then again, this was a spirit of the dead. He'd toyed with them before, in previous grindel research, and knew that they could toy with him just the same. What if she was lying to him?

"I want to trust you," he said.

The woman looked at him with big, moonlit eyes. "And you cannot?"

"I fear you are confused. You warned me to stay away from this creature and then offered to lead me right to it in the next breath. I've been tricked before while speaking to those on the other side of this life." He gritted his teeth.

"I want to trust you too," the woman replied. "You and your kin saw me die. You're the only ones who can stop the eyes from driving others to madness."

"Mad?" Nalor frowned. "Is that what happened to you?"

The woman sighed. "I … think so. My memory, it's like … a torn patchwork quilt."

"Hmm …" Nalor scratched his chin. Perhaps this creature, made up of 'the eyes', guarded Veil-Piercer, wherever it was. "Were you travelling north when these eyes found … uh … *saw* you?"

The woman focused on him, unsettled. For a spirit, her expression was ominous; her eyes were drawn together in so deep a frown, it was as though she'd seen a ghost herself. "That is something I cannot forget. Where to go and what I was doing there. Will you let me lead you?"

Nalor hesitated. He had no other choice, no better starting point. And they needed this grindel. If the spirit could get him close enough to it …

"Yes," he nodded. "Let us leave at dawn."

In the morning, Nalor assembled the crew, gathered downstairs, and paid for a bowl of awfully claggy oatmeal. Without a farewell to the Adiran hag behind the bar, he led the party out to the stables and arranged the horses. He hadn't seen the spirit yet, but he was counting on her appearing soon to ease the explanation he would owe to the others. He'd sat up for another hour after she'd departed, reading from a haggard copy of the Aobian *Book of Songs*. After some time scouring the words, he'd felt resolute that the spirit would help him find Veil-Piercer. The words from the page were burned into his mind:

Tala's initial report was recorded upon her return:

'My lost siblings in the north were felled by their own creation. I was told by a distant cousin who arrived at our tree, on the edge of supernova, that they had tried to pierce the veil between this world and the next.'

They were on their way as the sun began to spit its orange hue from below the horizon and the moon faded into daylight. The city streets were empty, and Nalor was glad of it; being in this hostile place any longer risked something bad happening to the crew. They were enemies, especially now that the war had ended. And at least until Therador won the next one.

The clanging of twin axes in time with hooves alerted Nalor to a man coming up behind him.

"Heard you talking in the night, brother," Scalmer said as they exited through the rear wall of Ghabbat, which looked up at a mountain, its peak touching the sky just like the spires of Therador's mountain range. What lay beyond, they would soon discover.

"I was talking, Scalmer," Nalor said. He wouldn't lie. Lying was no way to serve the earth. "I was talking to the woman, the one who died."

"From the tavern?" Scalmer asked, confused. "What do you mean?"

Nalor sighed. "Her spirit visited me in the night." Nalor squeezed his horse's sides with his legs, trying to put some space between them and the rest of the crew.

Scalmer sped up to match his pace. "I don't believe it," he breathed. "What reason did the spirit have to visit us?"

"She is bound to us by her honour," Nalor replied. "I thought it best to keep it quiet until she chose to present herself to the others. We all have meddled enough with spirits to know that they are intent on the promises they make. I trust her and agreed to allow her to lead us on this journey."

Scalmer swore beneath his breath. "What does a spirit know about our journey? Why did you not consult the rest of us first? Do you not realise the danger we face? The unknown?"

Nalor put up a hand to silence him. "Do you remember her last words, Scalmer?"

"The eyes. That was what she screamed."

Nalor nodded. "That is what she was scared of, what drove her mad. Whatever the eyes are, they caused her death. She claims they are part of a creature that is growing stronger. And she was travelling in the north. I don't know why, but I intend to find out. The spirit may be the passage we need to Veil-Piercer."

As though his words were some measure of the future, the spirit appeared before Nalor at that moment. He cried out, seizing the reins. The horse kicked into the air, crying out as the rest shied back behind him. "Dirt!" he swore, breathless.

"What are you doing, Nalor?" Veis yelled out from behind. "Steady on!"

"Sp-spirit!" he cried. "You nearly caused an accident!"

"Nalor!" Sachil roared next. "Move it!"

None of them could see her? "You choose to show yourself to only me?"

The spirit shook her head. "I will show myself as soon as you say it is time."

Nalor growled. "Well, there's no better time than now!"

"Who are you speaking to?" Talei called in that chiding voice he'd hated since the day he'd become a priest.

Then the spirit appeared, standing before Nalor with a brilliant blue glow about her, allowing her image to stand out against the light of the dawn. The whole team gasped.

"What is this?" Veis asked. "Nalor?"

"Brothers," Nalor started, turning his horse around to face them as his mother sidled up beside him. "This is the spirit of the woman who died yesterday. She says she will lead us to the north, where the thing that drove her to madness resides. It is there I hope to find Veil-Piercer."

"Fool of a boy!" Talei snapped, leaning over from her saddle and slapping him across the face. Nalor's cheek burned. Shocked, he cupped a palm to it.

"You don't understand," he insisted. "She knows the way. She is not like any other spirit. It is with us her debt lies!"

"For what? Killing her?" his mother shot back.

"That is correct," the spirit said, flitting between them. Nalor's horse brayed as the spirit passed through it. "You released me from the greatest madness known to man."

"We tried to save you! What tricks are you playing, spectre?" Talei said through clenched teeth.

"If I am playing tricks," the spirit began, "then I will be found out eventually. Please, take this, good lady." The spirit reached out with empty hands towards Talei's neck, but the woman flinched.

"Get away from me!" she cried.

"Mother, wait!" Nalor snapped. He didn't see her as his mother anymore, merely another servant of the dirt. However, he needed her to heed his call. This spirit was the key to everything they sought. He was sure.

Talei paused at Nalor's words, visibly surprised. The spirit slipped something invisible around Talei's neck, and moments later, a necklace, its chain blackened and crude, hung about her neck. The object took their breaths away: a purple jewel, oval in shape and glowing a faint violet, was set into a polished metal frame.

"This is … Luminous!" Talei said in disbelief.

A light that had been missing from her face for months, ever since they had lost Ka-Del, came back to her face. Something stirred in Nalor, too. A sense of joy at his mother's smile. He shut the feeling away into a deep part of his mind. The labour came first, not the heart.

"I feel … a quarter of my years," Talei said in a calm tone. "This stone …"

"What is this, spirit?" Nalor demanded.

"Something I found," the spirit explained.

Found? Nalor shook his head. She was not Aobian, though. How did she work with a Luminous material like that? "You found it on your travels?"

The spirit looked past him, like she was focused on some detail in the distance. Finally, she answered, "Yes. It had to do with my work in the north."

The tension in the air was so thick it could've been cleaved in two. The priests watched on, either resolute like Sachil or with a hand cupped to the mouth like Kai. This couldn't be a lie. The grindel around Talei's neck was really there.

"Tell me all you know," Nalor breathed.

"All I need to do," the spirit replied, "is take you there. Then, you can see for yourself."

She rose into the sky. Her last words became fleeting, reverberating as though they were spoken inside an empty hall. She began to move forth, and Nalor followed. The rest fell in behind him, and they were quickly on their way when they caught the next words she said.

"All that is left where we are going is life on the brink of existence."

PRISMA

Autumn's Heart, 2055 AS

I T HAD NOT BEEN an easy journey to the base of the mountain, where the river was, but Prisma had found her way there eventually, collapsing onto her bedroll that had been laid out upon the soft grass along the riverbank. The Tree stood over her like the ruler of the world, in a different way to Aobia. At home, she found comfort glancing up at the wide, green canopy that seemed to hug the earth it was planted upon. This Tree, however, was menacing. The leaves were needly and a greyish-green. The wood was deep brown with a crumbly and worn bark that showed its age.

She held her gaze on it from her position lying down. Something was missing from this Tree. There were no sounds in the air, no animals or birds. Barely any wind. All that she could hear besides her own breath was the water of the river. *That's what is missing,* she thought. *Life.*

"Water," she muttered, sitting up and striding to the river's edge. She reached down to cup her hands in the shallows before thinking twice. The water moved normally, but this close, she could feel an unnatural heat emanating from it.

The river in Aobia was sick, and she knew heat was one of the signs of it. Did the Sickness exist this far north? She desperately needed a drink. If sick water was to be the end of her after coming all this way, then the gods enjoyed too many cruel jokes. She felt the light flow through her, to her fingertips, and touched them to the water's surface before recoiling with a gasp. Sure enough, this water was not safe. She'd seen sick water before. Nischia had worked with the Water Management Facility in Aobia for a time and had tested sick water in the confinement of the branchtop laboratories. Prisma had visited her there once, with Loche and Koln, Nischia's superior, and had seen the water up close, illuminated with several *cism* so that the poison within was obvious. The nature of it was unknown, but the signs were often a mixture of heat, a strange frothing, and an acidity that wouldn't have been present otherwise.

Prisma continued to feel there was something cold and empty about this place. It was eerie to dwell on for long. The quiet of life around this Tree ... it was as though there was nothing here *at all.*

She looked toward the Tree that was standing in the river like a spear through the centre of a man's heaving chest. Studying the trunk, she realised there were sections cut out of the bark, like …

"Stairs," she breathed, taken aback. They must go on forever. Aobia was dependent on its lift systems, with the oldest sections of the stairs having faded into bark. She couldn't believe this tree operated with a simple staircase. Then again, maybe those who had lived there never needed to reach the land below. After all, recorded visits of these northern tree-dwellers to Ghabbat were nonexistent, based on the documents she'd tried to read in the archives there.

River water sloshed in rapid, tumultuous waves of foam and mottled blue past the trunk of the Tree and over dicey, jutting rocks. She would have to be careful not to fall in, as she didn't have enough Luminosity contained within herself to fend off the Sickness, and she wasn't sure how much submersion would result in it attacking her body. But maybe she could find the point on the trunk where the stairs began. Rounding the circumference of the Trunk on her side of the river took nearly an hour, and after walking carefully along the water, looking for points where she could safely stand or cross, she finally found a vantage point for the entrance to the Tree. At its base and embedded low in the water, a wooden branchrendered—no, trunkrendered?—gate marked the beginning of the stairs.

Relief overcame her but was quickly overwhelmed by her stomach growling. She searched her roll for evidence of anything remotely considered to be food, but all she could find were crumbs of dried cheese. *Think, Prisma. You need to get into that Tree.* Where was Tayriah when she needed her? Gods knew that falcon could nearly pick Prisma up with her claws and carry her straight to the top.

She routed some Luminosity to her fingertips, getting a feel for all that remained inside. A trickle as opposed to an open faucet of raw energy, but maybe enough. Perhaps, with some ambition, she could guide the water to push away from itself, creating two opposing waves that would allow her to step across whatever rocks were concealed below the surface and up to the gate.

Prisma outstretched a hand, letting Luminosity run from her fingertips, determined to part the water. But she wasn't confident in her ability to do something this grandiose, even if she had been fully imbued. Nothing happened to the water during her attempt, but she did feel something grab on to her hand like a magnet, a sensation similar to another hand. She yelped in surprise, retracting her hand. Something near the gate had responded to her Luminosity.

"What in the Canopies …" she breathed.

She reached back out, and the little amount of Luminosity she let flow was again gripped by the unseen source across the river. Somehow, it was using her Luminosity as a conduit. But to do what?

When she allowed the connection to remain between her and the source longer, nothing changed. She furrowed her brows, confused. Perhaps this was the way to open the gate? A sort of key that could be toggled with Luminosity?

She allowed the connection to remain open, and eventually, with extensive patience, something happened. Water parted, revealing soft earth, dead leaves, and rocks. It was as though the river flowed up to a point, skipped a few steps, and then began again.

Prisma ran across the small space, leaping over rocks until she was able to step onto a tiny wooden platform that formed before the gate. The second she let the Luminosity go, water rushed back in and filled the gap that had been there moments before. *There are more strange things about this Tree than I can put a finger on, and I am still only at its base.*

Looking up, Prisma studied the wooden gate. Two frames that could open outwards, made from Tree-wood, she was sure. The wood had been fashioned in such a way that the gates looked like thick vines had been wrought to form the shape.

She put her hands on the gate, warming it with the dregs of her Luminosity, and waited. Nothing happened. The source she'd felt moments ago, the one that had latched on to her to open the river, was undetectable. She couldn't believe this.

"Roots BELOW!" she snarled, fed up, hungry, and exhausted. "Just open, damn thing." She yanked at the gate, and it creaked, but it was solidly fixed into the trunk of the Tree itself. It wasn't going to budge.

Prisma ran her hands up and over the wooden gate one last time, feeling around the cylindrical patterns of interconnected wood, polished and buffed by the constant exposure to the elements. A soft glow radiated outwards from a divot in the wood, towards the top of the gate. She stepped up to it, eye to the divot, trying to make out what it was. Inside was an aura of purple, surrounding the faintest outline of a round object. *Maybe I can use what little I have left to retrieve whatever is inside the wood,* she thought desperately. It must have been the thing that had connected with her.

It was a toss of the coin whether this was the right thing to do, but the ground she stood on was dwindling as the river rose back up around the rocks. She had to act with haste. She sighed before closing her eyes and centring herself with a deep inhale.

"You can do this," she muttered, reaching for the final droplets of light within and directing them at the tiny divot in the wood, her index finger held firmly over it. Light moved like dewdrops falling from a leaf in the drying summer sun, threatening to vaporise, to expire.

Please! she begged. *Even if it means this journey will be the end of me, I need to open these gates!*

Just then, a fine purple glow sprayed out of the hole, and the wood expanded ever so slightly, allowing her to dig her hand in and edge the purple object out. Her eyes widened as she retrieved a small, glowing jewel fastened to a chain necklace. Light swirled within and around the jewel, and she could not tell whether it was the Luminosity she had given it or if it had already been there. "What is this?" she asked.

The gates squeaked open, and she slipped inside, stunned. The little jewel shone with a bright, joyous violet and was oddly warm in her hand. One moment, she'd been begging for the gates to open, and then she'd found the jewel ...

This was an oathstone, and she had exchanged oaths with it. Her life for the opening of the gates. "Even if it means this journey will be the end of me," she said, breathy with disbelief. The stone's light went dull and became cool to the touch. The oath had been completed, just as it had been described in *The Book of Songs*.

The climb up the staircase was staggeringly difficult as the stairs had begun to erode and the surface of the trunk flattened. With no grip and slippery, shallow footsteps, Prisma had to engage every muscle in her body to make it up to the first tier of branches without falling.

At the top, the first tier of branchroads spanned out before Prisma, a new world already in decay. The branchroads were rotting in places, grey and dry in others. Branchrendered homes were collapsed on roadsides, overgrown and dishevelled. This had been the home of an entire people, and Prisma's footsteps were the first to touch the same ground in a long time, longer, she presumed, than anyone in the Magisterium would have hinted at. Despite her hunger and exhaustion, she sat in the middle of the main branchroad that stemmed off the central staircase, taking in her environment before whipping out her journal and *The Book of Songs*.

The Aobian book was no help, its only mention of Tala's journey to the north being a brief paragraph before the history was interrupted by verse. A pattern of the ancient tome was its ebb and flow between poetry and factual recount, making it difficult to digest.

Prisma flicked through the pages, intending to set the book down soon, and stopped at a four-line verse on its own page without a title.

> *The soul within us all is shared,*
> *The land around is duly prepared,*
> *For life in its abundance to course,*
> *Like light between the heavens and us.*

At the bottom of the page, a single attribution was listed: *L.* Was this the author of the verse? It read smoothly, with a clear and intentional sequence and rhyme.

"This was never written in the Old Tongue," Prisma breathed. If it had been, the translation would most likely not rhyme at all. That meant this verse had been written in recent history, making it very interesting that it was in the book at all.

She took out her journal and copied the words down line for line, wondering if the page she'd accidentally stumbled on was present in other copies of the book. Then again, this had come out of the official archives for Aobia, suggesting that what the common folk had access to was not exactly the same text. What had the Magisterium selected for the people of Aobia to read or not, and why?

The soul within us all is shared. She recited the line as she closed her journal and repacked both books into her roll. There was nothing shared in this place. Giant, dry ochre needles matted the roadside, a sign of the Tree's slow death, and the musty smell of decomposition hung about as though the canopies pinned it against the ground.

She wandered down the street further before coming to an overgrown matting of weedberry that seemed to have consumed an entire branchrendered home and was dotted with tiny blue berries. Sour yet edible, the berries offered her a brief bout of much-needed succour. In Aobia, if anyone had weedberry growing in their garden, they would cull it immediately, dry it in the sunlight to kill it, and toss it away to decay somewhere below the Tree. Here, it was the only thing growing.

As she munched on the berries, she took in the architecture of the houses. Unlike the rounded homes in Aobia, these were more conical, sometimes multiple stories high, and always ending in a pointy annex, reminiscent of the Tree's actual shape.

A breeze began to blow through the branch, kicking up into an unexpected gale, and she struggled against the impact of it, running back to a vine-ridden home for cover. Suddenly, several quaking rumbles made the branch move, the house creaking as Prisma lost her footing. She squeezed her eyes shut, listening to the rumbling and thudding emanating from somewhere higher up in the Tree. Within minutes, the strange experience was over, and the Tree became silent once more.

She adjusted the necklace with the oathstone around her neck. The stone had changed colour, from a resonant violet to a deep blue. In Aobia, *cism*-powered appliances and machinery turned blue to let the user know they were nearly empty and required changing soon. She tucked it back into her shirt, wondering what the colour change signified for the stone.

"What in the roots below was that?" Prisma whispered, terrified. Then a click and creak sounded from behind her, and she whipped her head around, alert. The door of the weed-covered branch-home had opened in the strange quake, and her curiosity got the better of her.

Ducking inside the cold, dark home, Prisma squinted and placed her hand on the walls, feeling their rough, broken surface. The home was neatly arranged, but everything in it had become a broken, crumbling mess or was hidden beneath layers of dust. In one corner, a dilapidated bookshelf held a number of mouldy tomes, the covers of which bore titles and embossments that Prisma could not make out. In another, a mostly tidy kitchen remained intact but was covered in years of collected dust, an indication that whatever had taken place in this Tree, it had absorbed the life from it. One day people had lived here, and the next, they were gone. *These people were not slow in their decline,* Prisma wrote in her journal in the fading sunlight. *They were practically erased.*

She closed the journal and kept walking through the house. Something was making a low noise farther down the hall, where Prisma could see a single door closed. The second she placed a foot on the hallway floorboards, a sudden vibration shook the home, causing dust and debris to fall from the roof, which was broken and invaded by dried patches of the weedberry in several places. Though it was a branch-home, this roof had been affixed to the top, as though the whole home couldn't have been rendered from the Tree. Startled, she pressed on, determined to reach the door.

WE FOUND YOU.

She stopped, her heart thudding. A voice—not her own—had spoken in her mind. It felt menacing and aggressive.

The Tree shook again, like it had when she was outside on the road.

WHO ARE YOU? YOU SHOULD NOT BE HERE.

"Agh!" Prisma cried, moving her hand to her head. She felt dizzy, like the voice was stabbing her in the skull. She staggered down the hall, falling to her knees. The oathstone came loose from her neck and fell to the ground. It pulsed with blue light as striking as the morning sky. She still had no idea what that meant, but she seized it back up and began to slide across the floor. "Leave me alone. I come in peace, and I will go in it too."

GO? The voice asked, booming through her head now. The Tree trembled and Prisma could not climb to her feet. She slid down the hall with one hand along the wall and cupped her head with the other. She was nearly at the door, and amidst the chaos, the sound emanating from behind it sounded more familiar and sweet than anything else had in this Tree. It sounded like a song, like …

WE CANNOT ALLOW YOU TO GO. BUT IF YOU INSIST, YOU WILL GO IN PIECES.

She got to the door, turning the rusted brass knob and kicking it open. Before her, her Orb swelled, filling the room with light. She stayed on her knees, sliding desperately across the floor to her Orb. It had come to her, just like it had when she'd fought in the war.

Perhaps it knew the dangers she faced, or it simply identified her anxiety and was moved to be with her. It didn't matter the rhyme nor reason, though; her Orb was here now, and it was a safe haven. A place to refill and to Sleep. Then she could face whatever was out there, calling to her in her mind.

One giant quake caused the place to shift on itself suddenly, the beams of the roof collapsing over her. In what seemed like a second, she flung her roll off her shoulders and dove into the swirling glow of the Orb, fragments of rotten wood smashing onto the floor before her. She took up her position in the Orb and felt its dense, warm Luminosity flood her, silencing her mind, singing to her, welcoming her home …

YOU ARE ONE WHO SLEEPS? the voice asked, clearly surprised. *THEN WE WILL FIND YOU, AND YOU WILL BE OURS!*

Her mind fell to the song of the Orb, and everything terrible faded.

NALOR

First Frost, 2055 AS

IT WAS LATE WHEN the priests and Talei came to rest after struggling to ignite a fire in the failing light. Rest was interrupted often by the scuttle of creatures, but the darkness was a good companion for Nalor's anxieties.

The Aobian *Book of Songs*, however, kept him company between bouts of light sleep. He held the book under the moonlight and pored over its several thousand thin pages with the same devotion and studiousness he'd had since his ordination. Occasionally, clouds slipped over the top of the lunar glow and his eyes would close, content. Then, he'd be awake again, looking up at the bleak and steep climb to the peak of the mountain behind him, hearing the owls and other things only meant for the dark creeping through the grass.

The spirit hadn't been seen since they'd elected this place to camp, a decent mile or so from the mountaintop. The way had been difficult but not as precarious as Nalor had imagined; in fact, he was surprised to have followed a track through the mountains from the Ghabbatian hills where they'd set off that morning. Maybe more people than he'd realised went this far north. Maybe the secrets the mountain coveted were no secret at all.

Luminous things, The Book of Songs read, come from the heart of the land. Though we are not inherently Luminous, we have a way to become so. We must be Blessed by the Tree. That Blessing is only meant for a select few, and its origins are unknown. Tala would not speak of them, but I imagine she knew much more than me.

The chapter he read was from a shorter book contained within the text that held no songs or poetry. These were recounts from the diary of a direct descendent of Tala, the first All-Mother of Aobia. Tala was the one who had brought the tree-dwellers to the Trees for succour. They'd come from the Janub desert and settled on the fringes of the forests south of central Q'ara, which contained the expanse from Sethiliquin all the way across to Adira on the opposite coast.

If anything was to be learned from Tala or the generations that proceeded her, it was that they understood these Luminous objects with an affection that Nalor never could. He needed the facts, the science. They never did. They needed to feel connected to it, spiritually and emotionally conjoined. Perhaps that challenged the truth of what was recorded in these histories, but it didn't diminish it entirely.

Nalor glanced at Talei, who was asleep in her sleepsack, facing him. The necklace glowed dully. *Luminous things come from the heart of the land*, he thought, quoting the text he'd just read. It was ironic that despite the fallacy he saw in the tree-people and their over-reliance on a spiritual connection to the land, he could not deny they shared a purpose with his people, the Priests of Dirt. They were both tied to the earth and knew the importance of giving back to it.

Maybe they would reconcile one day. But first, the Aobians would need to bend to the might of the Empire. Without that, life on Q'ara would continue to be tumultuous.

The grim red of morning began to alight from behind the eastern wall of mountains, and Nalor blinked his tired eyes. So began another day.

He roused the others quickly, watering the horses and giving them their feed from a sack strapped to the side of his saddle. It was running low, and they hadn't even made it to their destination. He cringed at the thought of having to scavenge for horse food in the hills on the way back to Ghabbat.

Sachil was preparing a pot of oats with some berries and meatlife—rabbit—he'd foraged the previous day while the others packed their bedrolls and found a place to sit around the small campfire. Nalor warmed his hands over the flames, studying them, the heat of the licking flames reminding him of the grindel he'd seen shatter only weeks before. When that Kathani spear had given its all, it had lit up the Piatic Hall of the Dead like the sun, vicious and volatile.

He wondered how the spirit's killer, the creature with the eyes, could be connected to everything. What if the spirit was leading them on a goose chase and there was nothing to be found in the place she was taking them? Still, it was better than carving their own way through the mountains and hoping they'd stumble upon the secrets they sought.

A figure sat down beside him as Sachil began to plate up the oats onto flat wooden boards he'd packed. Nalor turned to look at them and was startled instantly. "Spirit," he proclaimed. "Where did you—?"

"You must hurry, priest," the woman said. "You must see what lies beyond!"

Those with spoons and those without looked, stunned at the woman's sudden return.

"Spirit," Talei croaked, clearing her morning throat. "How far is the top?"

The spirit blinked. "Not long, oathbearer. I found this path through the mountain myself as part of my research. I know it well."

Nalor shuddered. This woman... *she* had traversed the mountains to the north? Alone? Who was she?

"What exactly were you researching, spirit?" Nalor asked, taking a small amount of oatmeal on his spoon.

"Something that I will not share," the spirit said. This was the first time she'd pushed back on his questions, and Nalor felt himself losing control.

"Tell me, spirit," he commanded. "You said you were bound to me!"

The spirit began to fade, looking away from him.

"Spirit!" Talei cried. "Don't leave! My son, he is quick to anger, but he did not mean to threaten you."

Nalor shot Talei a look, his eyes filled with rage. But when he looked around at his brothers, none of the other priests shared his sentiment. Instead, their expressions were flat or resigned.

"Maybe I went too far," Nalor said, softening his tone. The spirit's visage returned to its full opacity, and he breathed a sigh of relief. "If you do not wish to share your research with us, spirit, you do not have to. I am sorry." He hung his head, and the ghostly woman nodded.

"You must know that if I was to die, those secrets would die with me," she said.

"You're already dead!" Nalor said, annoyed.

"Spirit," Talei said, interrupting. "What is this, exactly?" She held out the necklace with the Luminous stone.

"An oathstone," the spirit said. "My promise will not be broken. I will show you the way to the eyes because you freed me from their gaze. It can also be used for a warning. If something is wrong, it will … change. I learned that too late."

Nalor studied the stone, considering the change in colour it had undergone since the moment Talei had received it. It was still violet, but lingering in there was some cooler blue, and it seemed to be taking over as time went on.

"Please," the spirit urged, "no more questions. We must go!"

They ate and packed with efficiency, the sun still having not fully risen, before they got on their way. The steepness of the track was no small thing, and they each had to resort to leading the horses on foot. At the precipice, however, everything changed.

Atop the mountain was the expanse of the deep north, a place never chronologised or written about by any human settler. The crew moved to the edge of a short cliff, a slight outcrop of rock, where they could take in the skyline.

In the centre of their view, an enormous tree stood, alpine in shape, with thick, green tufts of firs on its branches. The trunk was thrust into the middle of a running river that terminated at a lake below them and headed out into the distance, beyond sight.

"A Great Tree!" Nalor gasped. "Impossible."

"Is this real?" Nalor heard Kai say from behind him.

"They're supposed to all be gone now, besides the one in the south," Scalmer said.

"It is real," the spirit announced. "And it is where we go. In it are the secrets of millennia, as well as secrets from another realm, a different place to this one."

"Different?" Talei asked. "To Q'ara, you mean?"

"No, oathbearer," the spirit replied. "An entirely different place. A place not at all like this earth. A non-physical realm."

Veis, Scalmer, Kai, and Sachil mumbled amongst themselves, but Nalor was fixated on the spirit's words. "What is in that place?" he asked.

"Two things," the spirit replied. "Two things competing for eternity, striving to eclipse or occlude. Light and darkness. That is all."

The Great Tree was a short walk away the next day, but they were parched from the constant movement throughout the night and equally famished. The river that ran beside them had come to a much more settled state on the flats that led to the Great Tree in the distance, and the banks were less treacherous to tread.

"I need water," Kai said with a husky voice. He shoved his way to the front of the pack and walked to the edge of the bank where the ground was muddy and filled with reeds. "The water farther out seems clean enough," he called to the others, and they nodded in agreement. Kai stripped from his cloak and top, casting them onto the riverbank with his pack and spear before wading into the river.

"We may stop," Nalor permitted. "But for no longer than an hour. The spirit has beckoned us to this Tree for a reason."

Kai nodded, before adding cheerfully, "The water is warm, brothers!" He ducked his head beneath the surface and was gone.

"Are you sure there are no Aobians in the north?" Sachil asked.

Nalor shrugged. "None of the histories have ever indicated such a thing. Perhaps they dwelt there once, but it is not likely now. How could they have lived on Q'ara for this long without us knowing about one another? We aren't more than a week from Ghabbat. People would have travelled these valleys."

Sachil seemed to accept Nalor's reasoning, taking a seat on a nearby fallen tree with a grunt. "Well, I need meat." He rummaged around in his sack, pulling out the leather wrap filled with dried rabbit. "Spare hare?" he asked.

Scalmer and Nalor took some scraps of the jerky, but Talei sat at the other end of the embankment, looking out at the Tree.

"What is it you are thinking?" Nalor said, walking to her.

"This hubris will afford us nothing but tragedy, child," Talei replied.

Nalor heard a splash and whipped his head around. Kai had fallen into the water, which had begun to bubble, froth forming on its surface around the place where he'd disappeared.

"Kai!" Nalor cried.

Scalmer dove in right away, dragging Kai to shore. The younger man was unconscious, and Nalor beat his back with a stiff hand as Scalmer leant him forward. Water came up from his lungs, spilling out of his mouth and down his chin, mixed with spittle. They laid him down, head over Scalmer's lap to keep him upright as Talei ran over with a rag torn from her dress.

"Here," she said. "It's soaking wet. Wipe him down." She clicked her fingers over Kai's eyes as Scalmer wiped the boy's forehead. "Kai, can you hear me?"

Sachil and Veis had crept over from behind, watching intently. Nalor cursed beneath his breath. There was no response. Kai the Bold was—

The river behind them surged like a wave out at sea, spraying water high into the air and breaching the caps of nearby trees. It crashed down, bits of it washing up on the shore, close to where the party gathered. It felt *hot* as it landed.

Nalor watched in confusion as his mother sported a deep frown, waltzing over to the riverside. "What is it, woman?" he asked, irritable. "Kai needs us!"

Talei ignored him, gazing at the river. "Something's wrong, boy." The necklace the spirit had given to her was pulsing with a dim blue light. It reminded him of Ka-Del, the spear they'd had that the Kathani man had ruined. All that time wasted for nothing.

Nalor scowled as he stalked past her. "Bring Kai, brothers. Sachil can carry him, and we can help where it's needed. Let's get to this damned Tree."

An hour's walk quickly became two, the men taking turns carrying Kai's limp body as they made their way to the base of the Great Tree. Its pine-like firs and greying trunk looked nothing like the Tree that framed the horizon when one looked southward of Therador.

They looked up at the massive tree, noting the top of it was lost among the low-lying mist in the valley. What was most curious, however, was the fact that the Great Tree was planted in the centre of the river, causing the water to split and fork around it.

Water pooled around the trunk, bubbling enthusiastically, and when Nalor reached his hand out from the riverbank, he felt heat emanating from the splashes. "It *is* hot," he breathed. "Like the Sickness of the south. Kai said it was warm!"

Talei stepped forward. "I know that Sickness all too well. Let me see." She held on to the glowing violet necklace, and as her hand drew near, the gem changed to a deep and resonant blue, like the colour of water on a starry night. "The very same. It must have gathered its heat once Kai entered," she said. "This is the water that took my people."

Nalor sniggered. "Your people? And yet my whole life you had nothing but regret for that old past."

"Regret is superseded by hurt, Nalor. Every time."

He wouldn't push her. He could hear in her voice the sound of stone ready to slam down on him. Sighing, he stood and straightened his back. "Why is it here, this far north? This is not the River Tomei."

"I am as bewildered as you," his mother murmured.

"So, Kai … will he …" Nalor gulped. Kai had worked hard for the earth and for others. It was not time for him to be reclaimed.

"He will die." Talei said it with no emotion, her eyes cold.

"Will your voice not even falter?" Nalor asked. "Have you no heart?"

Talei sniffed, shrugging. "He is not my spawn. Death is the way of nature. What more is there for me to say?"

"He's young, Mother," Nalor said, voice breaking. "It is not his time!"

"Is it ever anybody's time?" Talei shook her head. "Don't pretend you have any compassion for him, Nalor. Your heart is steel, as is his and all the priests'." She turned to the men behind her. Scalmer still cradled Kai, a cold rag pressed to the young priest's forehead.

"Get that cloth off him, fool!" Talei hissed, snatching the rag away and flinging it onto the grassy bank. "It's sick water, did you not hear?"

She bent over Kai, gripping his white cheeks and pressing firmly. When she let go, no colour sprang to the pressure points. Already, the life was seeping out of him.

"Where's the spirit?" Nalor asked. "We need her knowledge!"

"Lady Talei," Scalmer began. "What is happening to him?" The large man nodded to Kai, whose features were going slack. His eyelids, lips, and cheeks sagged to the side, as though gravity were pulling them in the direction Scalmer held him in. His hair became suddenly oily and seemed attached to his head like glue.

Nalor watched in horror as Kai's skin began to droop from his forearms, so low that it hit the ground like a dense, claggy mess.

Then, the young man's eyelids drooped, dangling from his face like the warm scrotum of a horse. The eyeballs, unbound, fell from their cavity and hit the ground, bumping lightly into Scalmer's knee on the way.

Scalmer yelped and reflexively shoved Kai away. "What in the dirt?" he whispered.

"It has taken hold quicker than I've seen," Talei exhaled. "This is … unfathomable."

Nalor bent to roll Kai over, but as he did, Kai's skin stuck to the ground, stringy like hot, melted cheese. As Nalor tried to let go of the man's arm, the skin stretched, sticking to his fingers. His body was collapsing now, thick blood oozing. The smells of excrement and spilled guts filled the air.

"He's gone," Nalor said under his breath. Then he turned to face his crew, speaking loudly. "He's been reclaimed."

PRISMA

Late Autumn, 2055 AS

PRISMA LEFT THE ORB the next morning, shaking and exhausted. That Sleep had not been conducive to restfulness. She held out her hands, inspecting them for signs of freshly imbued, silky-golden Luminosity.

There was none.

She gasped, putting a hand to her forehead. She was sweating, beads of salty water pouring down her head, across and into her hair like a river across land. She *had* Slept. She had felt the Luminosity filling her slowly, the Orb one with her, like she was used to. Nothing had felt *different*, and yet now that she was awake, nothing was the same.

WE WERE NOT EXPECTING YOU.

That voice, the aggressive one, boomed in Prisma's head, causing her skin to crawl immediately. She swooned but managed to stay on her feet. "What are you?" she asked.

YOUR SLEEP MEANS NOTHING NOW, LITTLE NOVA.

"Nova? I—" she started, but a jolt ran through her body like a spear, fastening her to the floor. She tried to scream, but only a hiss came out. Blood raged through her temples, and her hands and feet began to burn as hot as fire, the antithesis of life.

An image of eyes, thousands of burning eyes, flashed in her mind so intensely it was as though they were looking straight at her.

"The eyes!" she tried to whimper. The words barely made their way out.

WE ARE VEIL-PIERCER, AND YOU WILL FREE US FROM THIS PRISON, UNITY. ONLY YOU CAN. AND ONLY IF YOU BECOME ONE WITH US.

Then, a force like the wind that had shaken the Tree the day before coursed through the room and bowled her over. The air rushed back into her lungs, but her head struck the floor as she landed, and everything went dark.

Where am I? Prisma thought, staring into a darkness deeper than night. She was not conscious, not as she should be.

WE HAVE CONCEALED YOU HERE, UNITY. BE-
TWEEN WORLDS. BETWEEN VEILS. YOU CAN FREE
US FROM THIS PLACE. ONLY YOU.

Unity … she thought. *Why do you keep calling me that?*

BECAUSE THAT IS YOUR TRUE NAME. THAT IS THE
NAME INSTILLED IN YOU AT BIRTH WITH LIGHT.

At her birth? Then that meant … I was Named.

Prisma awoke in the dark with the echo of the words replaying in her head. *My name means Unity,* she thought, breathing rapidly. She'd been imbued with a Name at birth, a now-outlawed practice in Aobia because of the questions that came with it. Was a person truly free if they were forced to adhere to the meaning behind their name?

Loche's words came to her as she considered the things Veil-Piercer had told her. *I believe you are the only one called on this journey. You are the only one,* he had said. So the beast hadn't spat lies at her and this had been her destiny all along? Divide the creature and reclaim the souls it had consumed to reunite them in the proper manner?

She clutched the oathstone about her neck. Its faint glow allowed her to scan the room, which was empty. Even her Orb was gone. On the floor beside her was her bedroll, and Prisma unfurled it carefully, only to see the unread message Tayriah had brought her, back on the hike to the Tree. The parchment she had dreaded opening. If this was to be her time to depart this world, she could not do it without reading Altaea's words.

I saw your bird flying with the Greatbirds, he had written. She stifled a sob, hearing the nearby pulsing of Veil-Piercer's energy. "I knew it," she said, her whisper breaking as fierce sadness bore down on her.

She is a grand creature but bore no comparison to the ones she flew with, in size nor stature. I knew it wasn't one of our own. She landed to visit me. There was something about that bird that I could not place, but I knew that she did not come at your instruction. She came for someone else.

I knew one day, for better or worse, one of us would leave the other. I knew one day it would not last. We had no oaths to exchange, no donation to give, and no blessing from our parents. But for a time, we had each other. And that was everything. Everything.

One day, you may return. I hope you do, safely and with joy, once you have found what you were sent to discover. Our daughter still needs you. But when that day comes, know that I will not. Yet even though I may divert my eyes from you and act distant from you and request that I am moved to other clerical duties … no matter what I do, I cannot remove the part of me that is you. It is bitter, but it is true. My heart will never heal. And it will never be only mine again.

A.

Prisma wept in silence, her tears soaking the page, crippling the words and their meanings, as the shaking sound returned. All that trembling … it was Veil-Piercer. She had to make a difference somehow. Even if that meant giving up everything. If her daughter and beloved could find a little more joy in the world because *she* found the secrets of the north and kept them from hurting anybody else … *If this is my time,* she thought, squeezing her eyes shut, *then I will go. I will find this other realm where these souls crave to fly, and I will die freeing them.*

That was it. The resolve she needed came to her like steel, and she stood, scrubbing the tears away one final time and putting on her bedroll before heading out of the branch-home. Nothing could stop her from finding Veil-Piercer and vanquishing it. She knew her purpose now. She knew what she had to do.

She crept along the outer edge of the roadside, using the grass and weeds growing on the fringes to pad her footsteps.

WE CAN HEAR YOU, LITTLE NOVA. DO NOT BE DE-CEIVED. YOU CANNOT EVADE US.

The Tree shook again, this time knocking her off her feet. She was getting used to the constant jolts the creature sent through the Tree. But despite this, it only reinforced her fear of what the creature was and how it would present when they came face to face.

She continued to skirt the roadside and headed toward the staircase from where she had entered the Tree.

Suddenly, light engulfed her, and she became a prisoner of it, struck by its intensity, unable to move. She covered her face, trying to blink it away, but it only grew brighter, threatening to burn her eyes from behind the cover of her hands.

DO YOU SEE US? growled the layered voices of Veil-Piercer.

"*All* I can see is you!" Prisma cried. "What can I do for you? I have come here to discover the secrets of this Tree, and *you* are the single most undiscovered secret here. But I might not be able to save you. I am no deliverer, beast."

The light dimmed around Prisma, the ordinary twilight glow returning to the Tree, and her eyes focused as Veil-Piercer came into view, *rolling* towards her.

Dozens of bands of light, all suspended around one another like a great ball of fire, rolled down the branchroad towards her. The sight of them frightened her even more, however, when she noticed the thousands of crying eyes dotted all over the bands, the last fragments of the souls the creature had absorbed. This assembly of light and lament was Veil-Piercer, and it was here to take her.

DO NOT TRY TO DEFY US. YOU ARE OURS! Light spat from the creature with the eyes like a funnel, blasting at Prisma with the heat of a furnace. White-hot, raw light singed her robes, burning the edges off. Then the smell of her burned hair rose in her nostrils. She darted aside as another wave of the light shot at her. She had nothing. No Luminosity. No protection. Was this where she would die?

Veil-Piercer did not want her understanding of Unity, no; instead, it wanted to consume her, so that she could become a new set of eyes. If she was not careful, she would become one with Veil-Piercer.

Do not fear, a new voice said, coming to her in the chaos. Her eyebrows rose in fright as she continued to dodge the advancing

Veil-Piercer's attacks, unsure about the source of this different, quieter voice. Then, it spoke again. *You promised unity. Trust me to help you attain it. The oath is bound.*

Around her neck, the oathstone was glowing a vibrant blue, so deep and resonant it shone through her clothing. *That creature is afraid of me,* the jewel said to her. Prisma realised the oathstone had taken her promise of unity. And now, it was giving her a promise in return. Perhaps she could weaponise it against Veil-Piercer somehow.

"I think I understand," she breathed, taking the stone from about her neck. She could connect to it like she had when she'd first opened the gate to this Tree. The tether that existed between her and the stone had then allowed her to command Luminosity to split the river in two. Maybe she could do something similar now.

She aimed and threw the oathstone at Veil-Piercer. As the stone moved through the air, the Luminosity emanating from it illuminated the figure of a tall, Aobian male's body, standing between Prisma and Veil-Piercer. It looked like someone she knew, but she couldn't make out their details. Then the strange fleeting projection disappeared just as surely as it had shown when the stone kept sailing past it.

A surge, like lightning from a storm, came off the creature. Prisma held out her hands as though to catch the surging light, feeling a small quantity of Luminosity flood her insides for barely a second. If she opened herself up to it, she could wield the creature's own power, safely and in small amounts. Then the stone hit the creature with a sizzle and the beast roared, hundreds of voices screaming as one as it rolled back up the road and out of sight.

WE WILL BECOME STRONGER. WE FEED ON YOUR FEAR, LITTLE NOVA.

I'll do whatever it takes to free you all, she thought, running to collect the still-shimmering blue stone. *That is my promise; to free you and unite you with the place you deserved to go before you became this thing.*

She ran to the stairs, intending to descend them and perhaps escape with her life and find a way to conquer Veil-Piercer. At the top, however, was a fracture in the wood. She put a tentative finger to the crack and felt it give as she let Luminosity wash over it. This was the entrance to a branch-home! She kept her hand against the wood, her heart thudding as the wood creaked open. She looked at the sky. Darkness was descending. Against the dimming sun, a sudden and large shape was silhouetted, and a gust of breeze flapped in Prisma's face. She felt a smile tear through all the uncertainty, pain, and anxiety.

"Tayriah!" Prisma panted as the bird lowered onto her lap. It had found her, despite everything. "You precious thing. You found me!"

Tayriah clutched a note in her claws and dropped it as Prisma reached out her palm. "Inside, now," she said to the bird. The creature followed her with a jaunty hop through the branch-home door, and Prisma sealed it shut with the bit of Luminosity Veil-Piercer had passed to her. Darkness shrouded her and she whipped out the oathstone, which was shining a brilliant blue and cast enough light for her to see the bird and the space they'd entered.

Behind her, the branch-home stretched out into a hallway of indeterminable length, fading into darkness. This was no home, she quickly realised. This was a tunnel. She wondered what it had been for, but her curiosity was replaced by the eagerness to read Nischia's words. She held up the glowing oathstone to the parchment.

Every second, minute, hour, and day. It never ends. The fear of not knowing where you are, whether you are safe, or if you will return. I find myself mourning you before you have even gone. Please come home soon, sister.

N

That was it? Prisma scowled, throwing the letter down.

THEIR SELFISHNESS BARS THEM FROM TRULY LOVING YOU, LITTLE NOVA.

Goosebumps dotted Prisma's arms and crawled down her neck as Tayriah cawed beside her.

YOU ARE HIDING. BUT WE KNOW THIS TREE.

Leave me alone! she thought desperately.

WE HAVE SO MUCH TO LEARN ABOUT YOU.

Prisma gulped. *I will never let that happen.*

YOU CARRY WORDS WRITTEN ON PAPER THAT CAN TEACH US EVERYTHING WE NEED TO KNOW TO TAKE YOU FOR OURSELVES.

Prisma's eyes darted to her shoulder, upon which one handle from her bedroll was wound over.

"Tayriah," she whispered to the grand bird. "I must go deeper into the tunnel. I will write one last message to Nischia first. You must leave immediately and deliver it to her at any cost. Do you understand?" Tayriah cocked her head, and Prisma took it as agreement. She sat, leaning against the wall that had been open moments before, and unfurled her bedroll, taking some parchment and her pen and ink. The blue light from the oathstone hanging about her neck was just enough for her to see the page.

This would be the last message she'd ever send Nischia. She couldn't even begin to *think* about writing to Altaea. No, this was the only letter she had space in her heart to compose. She scribbled the start, getting down everything she needed to. Then, when the tears began to run from her eyes, she sniffed her way through to the end.

Please, heed my final words.

Nischia, there exists a plane between this world and another.

A place where the tears of the stars above fall onto us.

Somehow, we never noticed.

Twin soul of mine, I go to them now. I love you.

Goodbye.

She rolled up the letter and held it out for Tayriah to take. The bird leapt up onto her shoulder and clutched it in one claw. Prisma packed up her things quickly, but when she got to the ink, she paused. There was just enough for one more letter. *It's now or never, Prisma,* she thought. *You either tell him or you don't.*

An overwhelming feeling washed over her. It was the right thing, to tell Alt. She knew she was unlikely to leave this Tree alive. Whatever she could pass on to him would be her final words. He deserved that much. Quickly, she scrawled another letter, copying in the last few lines from the one she'd written to Nischia. It was all she had left in her to say. Not a tear fell down her face as she rolled up the parchment, handed it to Tayriah, and packed everything else away. Then, with careful wielding of Luminosity, she slowly cracked open the walls of the branch-home and let Tayriah through to the sunsetting world outside.

"Him first, Tayriah," she whispered. "Him first. Go!"

The falcon took to the skies, her silhouette strong against the orange sun. Prisma watched her go.

Then the Tree shook as the sound of something heavy approached, like a boulder rolling along one of the branchroads. Gleaming bands of light moved towards her with the speed of a hundred stallions, and all about them were a thousand determined eyes, the souls of the damned assembled into one horrific creature. The last remaining people of this Great Tree, trapped forever unless she could free them.

Veil-Piercer.

There was no time to close the branch-home. Veil-Piercer had seen her there, inside the crack of wood, with all its eyes. She turned and ran. The cascading sound of Veil-Piercer crashing through the wood and down into the tunnel behind her filled her ears. There was nothing else on the planet that she could hear.

YOU CANNOT OUTRUN US, UNITY. YOU WILL BE OURS.

She heaved breath after breath, running with all she could give. Thick, stringy spit flecked up across her cheeks as she felt her mouth dry up, the dead air of these centuries-untouched tunnels burning her nostrils and filling her lungs with lies.

LET US BE ONE WITH YOU.

The tunnel never seemed to end. She brought the final droplets of Luminosity to her fingertips and held them out on the wall, scraping the skin open as she continued to run. She had just enough to open and close a space, maybe two. If there was one enclosed chamber to be found, somewhere that she could rest, confuse Veil-Piercer, and take in a brief moment of solace …

That was all she needed. A few seconds to collect her thoughts and invent a plan.

As if the gods were with her, a wall opened to her torn hands, now bloody and shredded, fingernails broken and grazes carved across them. "Canopies above!" she gasped, diving into the newfound chamber. She put her hand on the wall from the other side, and it closed, wood expanding as though it were alive. Within moments, the sound of Veil-Piercer crashing through the tunnels could be heard and she held her breaths for a time that felt like hours.

Then, once she knew the creature had gone on in pursuit of her, she opened her bedroll, took out her journal, and ripped the pages out, one by one.

She would not let this creature know a thing about her. Not if she could help it. Next came the Aobian *Book of Songs*. She paused, reconsidering destroying such a pivotal, ancient tome as this, the key to her people's culture and traditions. But, roots below, it was the only way forward. *Protect the knowledge at all costs,* she decided. *Even if that means you die with it.*

She tore the book to shreds, letting the pages fall all over her legs and the floor of the chamber. She felt dizzy from the effort of doing so, more than she should have. Then the heaviness of the air became apparent to her, and she realised she had to get out. She was fully sealed into the room, with no circulation of the air besides that she breathed. She was going to suffocate.

She held out the oathstone, its blue shimmer projecting onto the walls and ceiling. She leveraged the Luminosity she had stored, but the wall would not open. She clawed at it, desperate for fresh air. Light still flowed through to her fingertips. Was this chamber only enterable from that one wall?

PERHAPS IT IS YOUR TOMB, boomed the collective voice of Veil-Piercer.

A mixture of determination and fear overcame her, and Prisma looked at the roof and let loose all the light remaining in her. Splinters of wood fell upon her, but she had achieved what she had hoped for: the evening sky was visible now, radiant stars painted across it. She clambered up and out to the surface, finding herself on a new road, one she hadn't yet embarked upon, with a collection of buildings running along both sides, like it had been a thoroughfare.

There is nobody left, is there? she wondered, half-ready for Veil-Piercer to reply.

It did.

YOU ARE CORRECT. THEY ARE ALL GONE. AND YET, THEY ARE ALL PRESENT NOW, WITHIN THIS FORM.

Blasts of furious Luminosity lashed at her, the heat so intense she thought her skin would melt off. She leapt through the air to dodge them, crashing onto the ground behind a knob of branchwood that acted as a temporary cover. The creature had found its way to her and was rolling towards her at full speed. She ripped off the oathstone about her neck, remembering that it had fended the beast off before, and threw it.

The oathstone was sucked through the swirling bands of light that made up the shape of Veil-Piercer and spat back out the other side, falling somewhere near a patch of bushes along the roadside. The creature roared in pain.

Light was gushing from the beast to her like waves, as though she and it were connected. The several thousand eyes of the afflicted souls trapped there howled in agony. *The eyes!* she thought. The ones who had been bonded with the beast in their remnant states continued to scream. The eyes of those forever-burning people cried tears of fire. Now the light was leaving her, flooding through Veil-Piercer in a symbiotic transmission of power.

Somewhere within the exchange of Luminosity between her and the creature, something changed. If the light itself had a central nervous system, something was prodding it. The light came loose from her command and bared its angry teeth at her. She lacked all the control she'd had moments before. It was as though the creature had taken it for itself. She felt the wrath, the fury, and the force of Luminosity taking her over.

Was it the beast sending these attacks at her or herself? Doubt flooded her mind. Using too much Luminosity carelessly could lead to a Sleeper burning to a cinder, a process known as supernova. Like that of a dying star.

No! she thought desperately. She was being attacked not only by Veil-Piercer but herself as well. *I am burning out. Help me, oathstone!*

Pain unlike anything Prisma had ever felt reigned over her, ripped through her, and overwhelmed all other sensations.

YOU ARE OURS! the eyes screamed at her, continuing to pulverise her with inexhaustible torrents of raw light. *YOU MUST BECOME PART OF US—FOR UNITY!*

I cannot give you that! she screamed, gritting her teeth. *That is not what unity is. You can be united in the next world. All the souls you have consumed … do they not deserve that?*

The creature ignored her argument. *IF YOU WILL NOT HELP US, YOU WILL BURN AND ONLY YOUR CORE WILL REMAIN.*

Veil-Piercer was right. If she kept forcing Luminosity from herself with such intensity, she *would* burn out. She would begin the process of supernova and slowly turn from a person to a remnant core. *You say I will burn, yet you would have me remain halfway between this world and the next, with you, an abomination?*

Veil-Piercer raged, the sound of several thousand venomous screams at once. Another wave of light attacked Prisma, tried to absorb her, but still she pushed back, feeling her body finally giving out. Then, with one last surge, she sent everything she had at the creature.

I am Unity! she said to it. *You are false unity. You are nothing but a collection of lives lost, trapped. But I ... I will bring your prisoners the salvation they deserve!*

She sent everything she had at the creature. It recoiled and shrank back and within seconds blazed like an inferno before rolling away, up the trunk of the Tree, and out of sight.

Fire burned in her, but she couldn't turn it off. She'd let it move from a flame to a forest fire, overwhelming all of her. The conduit her body usually acted as when wielding Luminosity could no longer be regulated. She was a perpetual source of exchange, and she screamed aloud into the night, withering away, alone and hundreds of miles from home.

All that remained were pain and the image of Veil-Piercer in her mind. Though it was only an image, it felt as though the creature was watching her, savouring her for a later time.

The eyes ... She pushed on both her temples, trying to erase the image. A cruel, purple glow came from the base of a nearby bush.

The eyes! She squeezed her eyes shut as she bent down to pick up the oathstone. This was her oath. Unity. No matter what. *I can't do it. I can't!*

Light burned her veins from the inside, scorched her heart, her mind, and her soul. Before she knew what she was doing, she was running.

Without control, without purpose, she ran from the Tree. Light pummelled her like flames, burning, but still she ran, a false hope that the perpetual motion of her would snuff it out.

She would run to her child and her beloved, and she would not stop until she reached them.

In this life or the next.

NALOR

First Frost, 2055 AS

T HEY LEFT THE POOLING stew that had once been Kai where it was, toiling the earth as best they could to give the lad some kind of decent burial. Nalor read the reclamation rites as the others prayed over Kai's ruined form that his soul would find peace in the dirt.

He never thought he would see his fellow priests shed tears, but Scalmer and Veis were the first to fall apart. Of course, Scalmer had been the one to bring Kai to shore, and Nalor could see the damage it had done the man to see their younger brother in dirt through to his end. Sachil was quiet at the back of the pack, until finally he burst like whitewater across boulders.

Talei, however, was as sombre as steel. "Oh, shut up, you louts," she snarled as Nalor concluded the rites. "The idiot should never have gone in the water without clothes on. It's nearly winter, for dirt's sake!"

"Do not speak of idiocy in the same breath that you mention a priest!" Nalor said, stepping close to her. "I'd soon enough send you to the dirt if you test my loyalty to my brothers."

"Of course," Talei replied. "Why does blood matter when you have dirt?"

Nalor scowled and stepped away from her, turning to the others. "It is time we moved on. Gather your things and let us be gone. The Tree is in our grasp."

The journey to the Tree was short but uneasy on foot. At one point, they had to make the decision to tie up the horses, a mile or so away, as the monumental pine's roots twisted and bent out of the ground, ridges as wide as roads, as tall as bridges, and as unsteady as a cart in floodwaters. Nalor watched the creatures as they left, conscious that they would only have food for a day or so. Their lines were long, but there was always a risk of entanglement or of some other creature to come prowling.

After several roots were climbed or passed under, they came to the river and Talei sucked in a loud breath. "This water could still be sick," she said. The enormous trunk of the Great Tree stretched into the infinite sky and felt so large, the human eye couldn't take it in. But what exacerbated the sense of inaccessibility was the white water rushing around the trunk, blocking off any way for the party to get close.

Nalor cursed. Now was as good a time as ever for the spirit to return to them. "Spirit?" he tried calling out to the air, but nothing came back at him besides the sound of rushing waters. "How can we access the Tree?" he asked.

Talei shook her head. "I don't know." She shrugged. "The Aobians who lived here would have had methods of doing so, but without knowing the time that's passed since this Tree has been abandoned, I would not know where to look."

As if in response to Talei's resignation, Veis pointed at the sky directly above them. "Look!"

Nalor craned his neck, peering through the sun-soaked canopy. Ridges were cut out of the Tree, like a stairway built right into its skin. Some had collapsed over time, washed out or eroded, but the structure generally remained. He followed the stairs to the bottom of the trunk, noting that they wound around the back of it. "This way!" he announced to the others, continuing past the river's edge.

They continued for another half mile or so before they saw the other side of the trunk. The water foamed wildly before a gate that was installed into the wood to protect the base of the staircase that rose up into the Tree.

Nalor was breathtaken by the sight, jaw dropped and mouth speechless at the grand design the original Aobians must've applied to this Tree over many generations. How many had contributed to such a thing and never seen the end of it in their lifetime?

He took a step towards the riverbank.

"No!" Talei chided him like he was a boy. "It's sick water. Do you not understand?"

A ripple in the air caused Nalor's neck to crawl. The spirit had returned. "Priest," the spirit began, "you cannot take your party through the river."

"What should I do, then?" Nalor asked irritably. She hadn't been with them for a while and now she appeared to lay down more useless limitations.

"Where is the young one?" the spirit asked, eyes wide with worry.

Nalor was caught off guard by her apparent care that Kai was no longer with them.

"Dead," said Scalmer, filling the hole of silence. "Help us do his life justice, spirit. Take us into the Tree."

"The Tree is sacred," the spirit whispered, her voice unnaturally rich against the river, like a chorus of tower bells. "You must treat it as such if I permit your entrance."

"You?" asked Nalor. "Who are you to permit us anything? Your job was to bring us to the place where you went mad. Once you take us in there, you may be free."

"No," the spirit answered. "I will not leave your side, not when I know what you may face." She zipped to the riverbank, looking uncomfortable. "Well, you are ready. In that case, let us begin. Oathbearer, hold your Luminous stone." She pointed at Talei, who obliged.

The spirit watched as the stone's light began to leak into Talei's hand, like slow, purple ink. "It is just like Ka-Del," she said, her eyes lighting up as she looked at Nalor. Maybe they had lost the

Kathani spear, but there were clearly more grindels to find on Q'ara.

"Spirit, what is the origin of this stone?" Nalor asked.

"That, I do not know," the spirit replied. "But I encountered it in this Tree."

Nalor sniffed. "Before we go in, do you not think it necessary to share with us what you were doing? Nobody else has found this place. Who were you, spirit?"

"I … do not remember who I was. But I remember the command given to me. Go to the north, past Ghabbat. Investigate the creature." She swallowed. "I found the creature. The eyes. They took me, too."

So this spirit was not Ghabbatian? He thought about her colour when they'd found her collapsed in the tavern … the way she had glowed so brightly before dying. She had looked so young, but she'd been tall. Her hair had shone with an odd silver about it, mixed in with mottled grey.

"You are Aobian!" Nalor whispered. Nobody else heard him over the sound of the water, but the spirit held his gaze. *Of course,* he thought. *Luminous Light had exploded from her dying body.*

"I … am," she said. "I remember now!"

"You remember?" Talei asked. "What about your name? What is your name?"

The spirit looked at her darkly. "Let us proceed to the Tree. Do not let go of the stone. Focus it on the direction of the water and clutch it tight."

Talei did as bid, and the spirit reached out a spectral hand towards hers. The second the wispy fingers swept up against the stone, the light caught their outline, bringing the spirit even more vividly to life. Somehow, she too was able to touch the stone, and the light from it began to pour out of her other hand towards the river.

The men in the crew watched, mesmerised, as the light grew so strong in golden radiance and heat that it *pushed* the water to the sides, making a path across the riverbed that led to the gates mounted on the Tree.

"Spirit!" Nalor cried over the odd whirring of the beam of light. "Are you alive?"

The spirit did not look at him, but she spoke, her voice amplified over the noise. "I am considered alive in many respects, because I did complete my burning. You are lucky I am with you, because only I found the way to open the gate. Go through and prepare for what comes next."

They moved through the light cast by the spirit towards the Tree, swinging open the broken gates where the carved staircase was. Nalor felt his heart thud in his head. He had been led here, to this foreign Tree, by an Aobian Sleeper.

The ascension up the stairs was tenuous at the best of times, as the carved staircase was barely cut into the Tree and at points, the height of the divot made in the wood did not allow for the party to stand at full extension. How several full-sized Aobians fitted up and down this staircase, Nalor would never know.

The spirit, however, seemed to read his thoughts and explained what she could. "When I came here, this was the only way into the Tree until I was closer to the low-lying branches. It took hours. It will take us hours, too. I suspect the bark rings on this Tree have shed, and that is why the staircase is so narrow. Constant exposure to wind and rain would have altered the shape of the cuts, causing the height change at various points. It is a process known as erosion."

"You said it was the only way until you encountered the branches," Nalor puffed. "What did you mean?"

"And no tricks, spirit," Sachil interjected from behind. "I'm running out of breath."

"Not long to go until the staircase ends," the spirit replied. "It connects to a tunnel network that moves from the trunk through to the canopies."

"Ah!" Veis screamed from the back of the line, and they all whirled around. He had slipped from the steps and was hugging the edge with his forearms, his hands slipping from the too-smooth wood.

"Scalmer, pick him up!" Nalor cried. The way was narrow enough for only one person to fit, and he couldn't get past his men to ensure Veis was okay.

Scalmer fell to his stomach on the stairwell, Sachil grabbing his ankles from behind. Nalor gripped Sachil around the waist, hoping the chain of weight they made was enough to allow Scalmer the leverage he needed to pick Veis up from the edge. With Scalmer wriggling about, trying to manoeuvre his grip on

Veis' hands so that the fallen man could scramble up the side, Nalor and Sachil could not move a muscle.

As Veis tried to make his way up, the weight of him threatened to haul Sachil and Nalor over. Nalor sucked in a slow breath, trying to keep his feet planted on the narrow stair, his hands locked about Sachil's waist. It would be like a cascading series of dominoes if Veis didn't make it up onto a leg soon.

Eventually, the fallen priest had a knee hooked back over the side and rolled over, pressing his body into the cut-out wall of the Tree in relief. "Thanks be to the earth," he puffed, and the priests took turns to exchange their own wheezes of relief and thanks.

From the front of the line, Talei allowed herself a thin smile. "Now that we are all safe and fixed by gravity, can we continue? The staircase ends just up ahead." She pointed in the direction of the canopy, where, sure enough, it appeared that the staircase ended.

The spirit emerged from thin air once more, nodding along with her. "Yes," she said. "The tunnels are nearby. Let us keep moving."

It was barely a climb before they came to a deeper recess of stairs that led up to a broken door, where only a third of it seemed to remain attached to lofty, rusted hinges.

"Follow closely," the spirit said. "The darkness is immense. If you stay close, you'll see the sunlight again in little time."

"Can't we light the way?" Sachil called out from the back. "I've got rags, and the drier firs would burn easily enough." He seized a few bits of dried pine fir and crunched it up in his hand. Nalor shook his head before the spirit spoke. He knew what an Aobian's answer would be.

"Fire is the antithesis to life, priest," the spirit shot back, clearly disgruntled. "I tolerated your fire when you were cooking your hunt. *Your meatlife!* But keep your burning light away from this Tree at all times. I will not need to warn you again, will I?"

"I …" Sachil started to reply, but his sentence died before it truly began.

"Good," the spirit said. "Then let us proceed."

Inside the tunnel, the bleak darkness was more than unsettling. It was unravelling, encasing Nalor with a feeling that he had to run, had to find the light of the sun, *now*. But he persisted, knowing the others would be feeling the same trepidation.

They rounded several bends, watching their steps as the stairs continued winding through the heart of the Great Tree. When Nalor stopped to consider where they were, he continually found himself taken aback. They were in an undiscovered Great Tree, a remnant of some ancient time when these Trees had been commonplace across Q'ara. Even when Settlement had first happened, nearly two thousand years prior, there had only been a handful of the Trees left. If this was one of them, there was no documentation about it that he'd ever come across.

Warm light began to glow through the edges of the darkness, and the spirit looked disconcerted as she kept moving up the stairs. "We are not near the exit," she said. "I know not what this light is, nor where it's coming from."

She stopped and hung in the air.

"Should we continue, spirit?" Nalor pressed.

"I-I remember," she stuttered.

"What?" Nalor narrowed his eyes. She was looking in the direction of the oncoming light. He could see nothing up ahead. *Something is amiss.*

"Spirit, what's wrong?" Talei asked.

"Grasp the necklace, oathbearer," the spirit murmured back. Talei complied, and the spirit pointed at the right side of the tunnel wall. "Focus it here."

As Talei held the necklace, its dull glow painting a faded picture of the mahogany-toned wall, the spirit nodded with satisfaction. "Yes," she said. "It is through here. Do not leave this spot, humans. I need to retrieve something. The light ahead is ... concerning. Something, or someone, is approaching."

She disappeared, and the light from further in the tunnel grew brighter, making Nalor and the crew squint. When the spirit returned, it was as though the sun itself was there, and an odd whirring was sounding.

"The eyes!" the spirit cried. "That's what lies ahead."

"Where did you go?" asked Nalor, his throat dry with panic.

"I ... remembered I had abandoned something nearby. My journal. I did what was right and destroyed it."

"Destroyed it?" Nalor screamed, enraged. The light from ahead was so bright now, it began to feel *hot* upon his face. He was sweating. "Why would you do such a thing? The secrets it must have contained, the things you learned—"

"Do not question my decisions, foolish priest," the spirit screamed back. Talei shrank behind them, and the rest of the crew watched uneasily, hands over their brows to control the light in their face.

"Did you remember anything, spirit? Anything we can use to overcome this creature?"

The spirit looked pained but relented, giving an answer. "My name. I remember my name. Prisma. I was a Sleeper of the Great Tree south of the Mountain Pass, where I fought with my people. I came here to collect whatever I could. I was sent by my mentor. We were … studying the lingering nature of supernova events."

"Supernova?" Nalor whispered to himself. This Sleeper had been studying remnant cores—Sleepers who had spent too much of themselves drawing on Luminosity, the light-power they were able to wield because of the Great Tree they lived in. What exactly had been her mission?

The tunnels shook, like the kind of earthquakes they saw in Therador on occasion. Dirt and bits of loose wood crumbled from the roof, dust clouds blurring the image of the spirit and dancing like tiny pieces of shadow against the oncoming wave of light.

"Quickly!" Prisma cried. "There is a chamber ahead on the right. We must go there and hide, lest you become another soul to burn, another pair of eyes in agony."

They ran, stumbling through the blinding tunnels and moving into the room she'd forecasted. Breathless, Nalor pressed himself up against the wall, the rest of the crew following his lead. "You said we would become another soul to burn," he began. "What does this mean?"

"The eyes are a collection of souls, fed on by one remnant core that struggled to stay here in this physical realm. Now, these souls act as one, fuelling each other in a cycle of burning Luminous energy, staving off the call of the next life. It is as though they are stuck in supernova, and the only way to remain is to consume more life. It doesn't matter whether that life is Aobian or not. I discovered that the hard way, and then, when I thought I would lose myself—"

The room shook again, the light bending around the corner from the tunnel-halls. The whirring noise grew greater as Prisma finished her words. "When I thought I would lose myself, I retained whatever Luminosity I could take from them and started the process of burning. When I reached Ghabbat, I died and became what I am now, a spirit that cannot burn. I am neither a remnant core nor a ghost. I am … somewhere between. Now, cover your face. The eyes are upon us!"

"Them?" Nalor asked. Even with both hands over his face, Nalor couldn't prevent the intense, hot white light from finding its way through the gaps in his fingers. He peered through them and felt his stomach drop at the sight of the creature that had entered the room.

Thousands of eyes, some faces and mouths, screaming collectively in bands of light. The bands were like rings, wrapped around themselves, moving gyroscopically, the whirring sound of them forcing itself into his brain. The eyes blinked, looking around as the entire creature, in the shape of a ball, rolled around the room, trying to find … something. It rolled more aggressively, even passing by the crew at speed, growing frustrated, its pitched collection of moans and wails overcoming the whirring noise of its energy.

Then, it came to stop, and the eyes all turned to stare at the crew up against the wall. Nalor watched between his fingers. The ring-bound creature rolled slowly closer to them. The thousands of screaming mouths around it opened wider, and then he shut his eyes. If this was the end, he did not dare to watch.

Prisma's words echoed in his mind, and it all clicked. *"These souls act as one, fuelling each other in a cycle of burning Luminous energy, staving off the call of the next life."*

This was the greatest grindel ever sought on Q'ara.

This was Veil-Piercer.

"What is that thing, Nalor?" Veis asked, sounding frightened.

Nalor shuddered as the light-being sputtered with life, rolling around the chamber again, a great ball. He knew the answer, and the spirit—Prisma—did too.

"Veil-Piercer," they both answered together, and Talei gasped.

"This?" she exclaimed. "This … *thing* is the greatest of all the grindels on Q'ara?"

The creature bulged, several eyes expanding and blinking as the light of its rings swelled. It made a sound like a windstorm when its rings relaxed and moved apart from one another. The open space was like a mouth hosting a void within it.

"Slay this being and I cannot anticipate the catastrophe that may befall you," Prisma said over the snapping contortions of sound coming from the creature. "But defeat it nobly and find a way to contain it, and you will have access to the greatest accrual of Luminosity we have ever seen."

Hungry with anticipation, Nalor rushed to the other side of the chamber as the rings that made up Veil-Piercer rolled towards him. "What should we do, spirit?" he asked.

"The oathbearer must take control, harness the light within. Free those damning souls trapped within the celestial spheres of the creature."

Talei squealed as Veil-Piercer hummed past her, clutching the gemstone necklace Prisma had given to her. Some eyes at the end of the spinning ring that passed her seemed to jump in and back out of her chest, and Nalor watched in fright as his mother temporarily lost the momentum to breathe. The eyes had *gone inside of her.*

"Do not let them enter you, oathbearer," Prisma called, "for that is one way to go mad. Use the necklace. Hear its call. I know you can do it. I gave you the necklace for a reason. It contains in it a piece of me, my true nature. Unity."

"A piece of you?" Nalor asked. Scalmer the Wulf stood beside him now, axe raised in defence as though it could stave off the vibrations of the oncoming Luminous creature. Behind him, Sachil and Veis ducked, unable to contribute anything. The creature didn't seem to respond to touch, but they felt it when it came near.

Prisma flitted over to Veil-Piercer, stopping before it, and the creature ceased its rolling. The rings rotated with their whirring noise in place, and the eyes all along them watched her intently. They could see her.

"You cannot take me," she yelled at the creature. "I am not with this place, not anymore."

The creature chirped like a thousand birds, the eyes studying Prisma's spiritual form with curiosity. Nalor gulped down the terror he felt at the sight of the unknown creature, watching as Prisma continued to speak to it.

"This oathbearer carries a Luminous stone. She will take your insides and gut you, consumer of souls. That oathstone contains your fate."

The rings shook more violently as mouths all over the creature opened, screaming with hot, venomous rage. Still looking at the creature, Prisma called out to Talei, who sat against the wall, panting.

"Now, oathbearer!" the dead Sleeper cried. "Like the water we parted, you must open the faucet from which Luminosity can spill out. Let it wash over you, like a wave! Only you can do it. Only you!"

Veil-Piercer rolled through Prisma's visage, and Talei screamed. "It's not working! I'm trying, b-but ..." The creature neared her. The gemstone she held so tightly was a grim blue now, the colour of warning. The colour of impending doom.

"Your mind … so closed!" Prisma cried. "Calm yourself. Steel your anxieties, keep them at bay like your enemies. You must, oathbearer. You *must*."

Prisma's insistence spiked a deeply buried fear in Nalor's gut, and he swore. If his mother was the only one who could use the Luminosity locked away in that stone, it was up to him and the men to keep her safe.

"Brothers," he said with a shaky voice. "For Kai and for all those we've lost, we must fight. Distract the beast. Our survival, and perhaps the survival of many others, hinges on this. Remember, men, that you are dirt."

He got to his feet as the other three responded with the words he knew they would carry with them to the day of their reclamation. "And to the dirt we must return."

Nalor drew his spear from the holder strapped across his back and knocked it against the wall of the chamber, causing the rings to revolve backwards, upside-down eyes gazing in his direction.

"Celestial creature," he called. "It is not her that you want."

Scalmer roared, holding his twin axes in front of his chest. The other two were ready with their spears, too, standing as one as Veil-Piercer rolled forward. It screamed with the sounds of the dying and zipped towards them, a streak of light following in its wake. Nalor could only see Talei fumbling with her necklace as he dodged the light-being, its hungry mouths crying out.

Sachil and Scalmer dodged in the opposite direction, and the three men regathered at the other end of the chamber as they quickly realised Veis was trapped, pinned against the wall.

"Veis!" Sachil cried, running back to the celestial creature. "Stop! Leave him be, beast!"

It was too late. Veis' screams were haunting. Nalor felt bile rise from his stomach, curdling in his throat. The priest once known as Firm broke into shards as if he was made from the same wood as the Tree, exploding with light bursting through the cracks in his shattered frame. Then, Nalor swore he could see new eyes, hot with fear, whirl around in the rings. There was nothing left of Veis except for a smear of black, sticky blood on the wall and tattered remains, like ash, raining down onto the floor.

"No," he breathed. This was not a just reclamation. Veis deserved to go back to the dirt, not be taken into some in-between realm of existence, forever tortured, forever a link in the chain of consumption this creature fed itself from. Nalor felt rage bubbling from within and held his spear over his shoulder, tossing it at Veil-Piercer. The spear disintegrated, blazing red hot and melting into the creature on impact. The heat of it singed the whiskers on Nalor's chin, and he felt as though he was in a blacksmith's forge.

They were out of options. Talei cried messy tears in the corner of the room, the spirit of Prisma trying to comfort her. Access to the Luminosity was contained within the oathstone. Veil-Piercer zipped to the sides like a boulder that had the mass of a cloud, crushing Sachil, his body alight with burning, yellow streaks. He cried out and was gone before Nalor could take in the final tragedy. Scalmer slid out of the way, stumbling and falling forward onto his axe. Impaled, he groaned. The axehead had split his stomach, blood and other mess dripping out. Veil-Piercer touched the edge of him, absorbing him too, the axe growing red hot. He was gone in moments, like it had never happened, like the Wulf had never existed.

Nalor had little left besides a useless, sobbing mother and a spirit who could do nothing. All he could do was hope that Veil-Piercer could not outrun him. He circled the perimeter of the room, a hair ahead of the Luminous creature rolling around his trail. He was out of breath, his lungs burning from constant movement in the hot and heavy room. Then, suddenly, Veil-Piercer stopped, and the whirring noise that accompanied the constant rotation of its rings grew louder, so loud Nalor could not hear himself think.

The eyes. The eyes studied him, their final victim perhaps. Veil-Piercer began to swell, the outlines of its image blurring, projecting scorching hot white light throughout the room.

Nalor felt the heat tugging at his skin, asking it to come off. Sinew revealed itself, and he watched in horror as blood pooled on his surface. Heat filled his mouth, startling his lungs, causing him to choke. An eye tore from his widening socket and rolled forward. His spine broke, his toes snapped, his ribs expanded as light bent them out of shape. Fluid rushed up his neck, into his skull, compressing his brain.

In his final moments, he heard the voices of thousands screaming at him to join them, to let go, to become fuel, to persist, persist, *persist* ...

CONSUMPTION

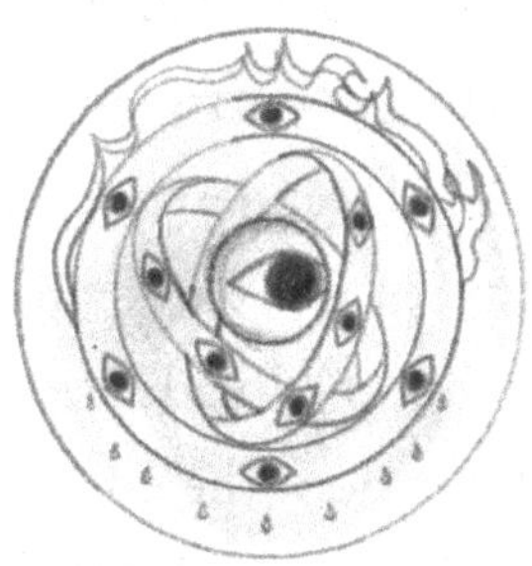

EAT. FEAST. THIS IS OUR SURVIVAL. THIS IS OUR PAST AND OUR FUTURE.

All around, light danced in swirling motions, an odd whirring noise filling the chamber. Finally, they would be unleashed. Finally, the greatest being on the earth would take its fill of the pathetic life that existed outside of this place. They purged the pain from their list of responses, clearing the instances that they felt the pricks of damage from those who had come to harm them.

Consumption happened slowly, but the light blossomed. There was only one left who would not be taken into their fold. They tried, but the woman refused to go. What did she know of them? What did she know of the burning they had endured for so long?

That thing about her neck was the source of her containment. That was the reason they could not look upon her and see the constitution of her mind break. It held an aspect of what they once were, and it challenged them. A natural source of light. It was a promise between her and the other one. The spirit.

Their heart was a realm of pure starfire, protected by the chain of souls they had ingested. A self-perpetuating cataclysm of all the light in the world. An Orb of Luminosity, taken beneath their wing, controlled immeasurably by the constant explosions of lightrendered souls.

The inside of the cavern was dark, and now they could see the light of the earth that they had been shut off from for so long seeping through the door the consumed ones had made. The tree-dweller who'd brought these beings here might not have been consumed, but she had been the conduit for their escape, nonetheless. They watched her fleeting spirit looking over the woman who was lying on the floor, blood streaking her hair.

That spirit was meant to be theirs. She belonged with *them*. *SHE IS OF THE TREE.*

But the spirit was also protected because she had passed into a different place. *WE NEED HER IN OUR FOLD.*

They cried celestial tears, feeling their connection to the physical earth sever as they were swept into a new plane, a place so far away from matter and time, they couldn't contemplate the change.

The spirit left, somehow manifesting a grip on the woman's arms using the power of the stone about her neck. It was over, unless they could consume more. *CONSUME ALL.*

They shivered short, sharp breaths and felt their great light fade. They needed to *consume*, but here, there was nothing save for black infinity. Here, they were the only light in the sky.

They knew they could only burn for so long. They knew it was time to consume their own fuel, every spirit, every offering that made them what they were, down to a final cinder. One day, they would expire, and they would feel the cold, grey weight of nothingness come over them forevermore.

NISCHIA

Epilogue - Winter, 2055 AS

THE QUAINT, BRANCHRENDERED HOME on the edge of the Soul was picturesque and peaceful, but Nischia felt the urge to turn back and go home grow by the second.

But I need to do this. For my sister, she thought. A mixture of feelings rested in the pit of her stomach. Surprisingly, the worst one sat at the top, leering at her even more than the grief or heartache she felt at losing Prisma. Betrayal. Anger. She was never supposed to know this male, Altaea. Prisma had kept him secret, even from her. That was what hurt the most.

Guilt tugged at her; she should never have stolen that second note from the falcon. It was not her business. She sucked in a breath and knocked on the door, which was rounded off in an arch, recessed perfectly into the home.

Nischia stood there a while before trying again. It was early in the afternoon, and the cool breeze of autumn's dying moments washed over her like a blanket of concern. Again, nobody came to the door. She gritted her teeth and pulled out a *cism* from her robes. Pressing her hands to it and drawing some Luminosity into her, she closed her eyes and sensed for someone inside. She hated probing for minds at the best of times and was glad it was not a common occurrence. This aspect of her power as a Sleeper was the one that left the most bitter taste, because it exercised her authority over the people.

She focused deeper, feeling the world fall away, replaced with only darkness. Usually, minds nearby would light up like distant lamps and she could move to them, in a sense. But there was nobody here. The closest life she could see was further down the street, and she detested herself for checking who they were. A young family of Aobians enjoying dinner together around the table. *This is not yours to see, Nischia,* she thought, chiding herself. She cut the connection between her and the *cism*, feeling suddenly cautious, though she could not describe why. Nischia had not Slept recently, and the Luminosity remaining in the single *cism* she carried was all she had at her disposal.

Nischia walked around the front of the building, unable to glance into any windows, thick navy curtains falling behind them. There was no glow inside, and the light of day was quickly turning into its own curtain of navy. She had to get in there. Something in her gut told her that this was not normal.

A cry sounded from inside the home, and she jumped at the sound. So there was somebody here? Why could she not see them? Were they ... shielded?

Nischia rested her hand on the keyhole and placed her other hand on the *cism* back in her cloak. She coursed light slowly through her until it reached the keyhole. Closing her eyes, she used the light to sense the shape of the lock and to fill it in as perfectly as the right key would. Typically, this was an illicit use of Luminosity, but she'd been involved with investigations with varying degrees of severity a lot over the years, and sometimes that allowed for channeling outside of the law.

She held her breath enough that her body stood still, allowing the light to bend its way into the grooves of the lock without being pulled slightly off course. Finally, it clicked, and she sucked in the fresh, cool air of the evening before opening the door and stepping in.

A gasp escaped her the second she tapped her imbued fingertip to the lamp closest to the door. That cry again! She moved through the house, her skin crawling with confusion, and the crying grew louder. *It cannot be.* It was behind a door in the hallway, and she turned the knob—

"No," she whispered. "A baby?" She stood paralysed at the sight before her. An older baby, perhaps a year or two old, sat in her cot, tears streaming down her tiny face. Crystal blue eyes, blonde-silver hair. *Like Prisma's!* She moved to the child, shushing it as gently as she could, but the infant only began to cry louder and then screamed.

She shook her head. Who was this child? It could not be Prisma's. It could not! She strode out of the room, trying to calm herself, to think away from the noise. She had to do something with this baby. She had to tell Loche. Canopies above, *she had to tell Loche.*

"No!" she cried as she took in the sight that came before her at the back of the house, before several bookcase-lined walls. "Not you! Not this!"

She clambered down to the floor, where the body of a male lay while the baby cried in the background. This was Altaea, and she realised as she studied his face, drained of pallor, that she recognised him. And she knew straight away why Prisma had never shared his existence with her. Altaea had been one of the clerics assigned to scribing for Loche, Prisma's superior, at magisterial sittings. If he had known about Prisma's love for the male, she could have been tried in the courts for a lifetime of imprisonment or exile.

Her head pounded with the sound of her heart racing like a drum, like a tide. Still, the child screamed. "Just let me focus!" she cried, slapping herself across the face lightly as if to wake herself from a nightmare.

Blood stuck in dry clumps over his arms and torso. She cupped his cold cheek and held his wrist, hoping for *something.* He was lifeless.

Nischia grabbed the male's other hand, unfurling his clamped fingers to reveal the bone handle of a hunting blade. A thick lump rose in her throat, and tears burned the edges of her eyes. Altaea had been dead no longer than a few hours, she estimated. The reason he'd cut his wrists was obvious, too: beside the body, a scrunched sheet of parchment rested, stained red in places. But she recognised the handwriting.

She seized the parchment and studied it closely, deciphering the words through the blood.

Altaea,

There exists a plane between this world and another.

The baby was wailing now, a vocalised version of what Nischia felt on the inside. Tears rolled down Nischia's face. This was the same message she had received herself. If only she'd known this male, she could have stopped him from—she could have had *somebody* to confide in, to grieve with, to—

A place where the tears of the stars above fall onto us.

Somehow, we never noticed.

Heart of mine, I go to them now. I love you.

Goodbye.

THE END *of*
THE CELESTIAL TEARS OF DYING LIGHT

Thank you, Fellow Tree-Dweller

Nothing fulfils me more than getting my work into the hands of readers. If you wouldn't mind leaving me a review on Goodreads and Amazon, (or if you can't, a star rating would also be fabulous), I can do exactly that. Reviews are like water in the desert, a way for me to keep writing sustainably.

Thank you so much for reading *The Celestial Tears of Dying Light*! Not only is this the final novella in *The Song of the Sleepers*, it is also the first to *not* be considered an entry point for the series. I've intended it instead to satiate those waiting for *An Empire of Dirt & Lies,* as a sort of lore deep-dive. The tumultuous happenings on Q'ara, however, are not over. To stay up to date with me and my work, please check out my mailing list at:

www.joshuawalkerauthor.com/subscribe

You'll find a companion narrative to this book, *The Rest to the Gods,* over there, too.

May the Light go with you, fellow tree-dweller.

Josh

November 2025

Acknowledgements

I start this acknowledgements section with a sigh of relief, mixed with an anticipating inhalation. With this novella, so much has been put on the table for the rest of the series. This era of prequel material is finished, and that feels good to say. Now, it's time to get back to the meat and potatoes, the last two books of the trilogy.

First and foremost, for guiding me through my most time-poor year yet, I have to thank my Creator. It hasn't been easy getting this book out there within the same year as another, but here we are.

To Alice, for being by cheerleader as I go into what I call 'crunch-time'. This series is moving ever-faster towards its end, and that means I have had less time for you and the things we love to do together as a result despite me trying hard to turn that around. Somehow, you still stand by me. I love you.

Similarly, to my family, who have both gotten me back to Sydney in the past year, but probably seen me less than when I lived eight hours away as a result of my new job and this writing stuff all being so demanding—thanks for keeping up.

To my beta team, let me preface this sentiment by saying that this finished book is genuinely so far removed from the beta copy, it's kinda crazy. And in part, this is thanks to your insightful reading and comments. Not only did you get me rethinking the possibilities for this story, you also helped me move closer in the direction I want to take this series. Thank you Carina, Isaac, Justin, Kris, Kenneth, Vivian, Nicholas, Ben and Amina.

To the Break-Ins, you indelibly remain my most important family in this bookish place. Scott Palmer, Rob Leigh, Isaac Hill, Kaden Love, Adrian M Gibson, Louise Holland, Calum Lott, Jonathan Weiss, Sam Paisley, Bryan Wilson, Francisca Liliana, Andrew Watson, ZS Diamanti, Nicholas W Fuller, Aaron M Payne, and Jeff Brown—we're two years old, and they don't call them the Terrible Twos for nothing. Let's keep rocking this boat!

To Sarah, my incredible editor, and Isabelle, my ever-dependable proofreader: the end product that the readers are holding in their hands right now would not be anywhere near as polished without your combined talents. Thanks for sticking by me!

To my cover artist Stef: Well, damn. I'm sad that this is the last novella in the series because I know that means for now, our time together is up. Let it be known now, however, that I *absolutely* intend to work with you again, when the time is right. You've truly helped bring this series to life, for so many people. It's a testament to your work that *The Rest to the Gods* remains, despite its short length, the most likely entry point for new readers. And *this* cover? Well, this one just blows the rest of the competition away. Thank you so much.

To my awesome cartographer Josh Hoskins, who captured the continent so perfectly. I'll be hitting you up in the near future to add some pretty important details to our map of Q'ara. Please remember me when you become famous!

To the online community of readers and writers online who have rallied around me, even when I've been a ghost, or when I've been feeling unsure, thank you. I won't list you all off here because it would truly be an inexhaustible list. Just know that I appreciate every. Single. One of you.

Lastly, to you, dear reader. I know I would have written *An Exile of Water & Gold* whether I had readers there for me or not. But this one, and the rest to come in the series? No chance they'd exist without you all. Please keep reading, and telling me about your experiences. Those moments are the most gratifying and validating for a new author like me. If you can do that, I'll keep writing. For you, now.

ABOUT THE AUTHOR

Joshua Walker is a fantasy author currently living in Sydney, Australia. He works as a primary school Literacy Coach, and likes to read, brew beer, and hang out with his wife and BFD (Big Fluffy Dog) in his free time.

To find out more about The Song of the Sleepers series, click here.